# NORMAN THOMAS

## The Thousand-Petalled Daisy

# NORMAN THOMAS

# The Thousand-Petalled Daisy

Published in 2003 by
The Maia Press Limited
82 Forest Road
London E8 3BH
www.maiapress.com

ISBN 1 904559 05 0

A CIP catalogue record for this book is available
from the British Library

Printed and bound in Great Britain by Thanet Press

'Everything there is,
is truth,' says Shankara.
'Everything else is false.'

# 1

# THE CAGE-BUILDERS

WHEN I FINALLY GOT CAUGHT UP in the roaring surge of the crowd I found myself chin to ear with a man smeared in ash. My chin, his ear; both as it happened covered in wispy hair.

'What's up?' I shouted.

I was standing on his dhoti and he was more concerned with tugging and clutching and keeping his dignity and his balance than he was in any answer. But he knew what was expected of him.

'It is all illusion,' he said.

Then I was hit by a brick.

When I opened my eyes he was still there, bending over me in a blur of light like a saint. He looked at me with concern, his cold black fingers touching my eyelids.

'Where is your mother?' he said, as if adding up my years.

The crowd, pouring forth sound like a storm at sea, had made a little pocket for me to fall in and when I had fallen into it had turned away as if tact or delicacy decreed it. I sat up and looked down into my hands and they filled with blood. The stuff was very red but everything else was losing colour round the edges and I slumped back to the ground, staying aware just long enough to see my decorated friend get hit by the next brick. It caught him behind the ear and he fell across me so I had a good look at his lump. It looked pretty bad so I expected to see him again when I awoke the next time crisp and white in a bare buff room smelling of mouthwash. But he was pretty black even for a South Indian and smudged besides and so they probably just rolled him round the corner. Anyway, rolled or left or segregated, he was nowhere in sight when I looked out at the world again, which was a pity for I'd lost a lot of blood and could have conversed with him on his own terms.

They are interesting, riots. I have seen a lot of them. You might even say that they have become a kind of family tradition. At least it has always been considered the thing to do. Even when I was still in teeth-braces and red, white and blue tennies I always felt I understood them. I certainly never had any illusions about them. I knew as soon as you drop your poster and everyone starts running no one cares any more what it's all about. All it is then, really, is that eager huffing-and-puffing, back and forth down alleys, around the back of supermarkets, giving vent, whatever vent is, giving vent, rocking a bit of London Transport, bending a bit of glass.

But in any case Indian riots are something else. Like no one is going to smile at an Indian cop and put a daisy down his gun barrel: he's just likely to blow it clean through your head. When you are new here seeing someone sitting against a wall fumbling his fingers in his banana-leaf plate you just can't believe he could find enough stuff to whistle a tune leave alone riot. And you can see he's easily bullied and can't get organised too well. Then, he panics like a shrew in a bucket. But he has one advantage: he can gather into pretty big crowds.

Of course the ones who make the most fuss are always the ones in the middle where no one can get at them. The ones on the fringe, nearest the lawnorder, often look as if they have just realised they've been queuing for the wrong bus. Now them the cops love: they're just the thing to make them forget that they've missed their mid-morning tea.

But this one I felt really didn't have much to do with me. This riot. After all I'd just arrived. I mean I'd just got off the train from the north, pooped out and sick. I was still carrying my kit, hadn't even found a bed. There was all this laughter, people taking my arm. We shall overcome, someone said to me as if he'd thought I'd written it and wanted me to know he thought it fitted the occasion. The whole thing was a puzzle, before and during. Afterwards of course it was different. Afterwards you could sort it out, taking the people out of the situation, the danger out of it, the fear out of it. You make it a custard-pie-in-the-face bit of business and it becomes a different story altogether, one that though it may not be true is the one you can live with . . .

Do I always talk like this? Listen, I've been sick. You can overlook anything, can't you, when someone's been sick. And as the man suggested: I'm just a boy. Can't vote, can't drink, need permission to say I DO. But between you and me I think someone lied about my age.

13

Anyway ever since I stopped the brick, though I know it's no illusion, nothing much seems real either.

Like now, this moment.

The river is there, a warm wet fact, flat and wide, muck-green, slow-moving. And the boat, leaky, jerry-built, that too is more-or-less real. But my relationship to the boat and to the river seems tenuous, to say the least, subject to whim, governed as much by this as by that. Neti, neti, so to speak.

A sheet of coconut matting had been rigged up to cover me in a dappled shade; the others sat in the sun. Martin Solar, my doc, in his white soft hat with a clam-shell brim, was turned towards the shore but looking downstream to where the river seemed to end in a field of reeds and water lilies. But the end of the river was also an illusion, the low bank hiding a turn in its course.

The Indian boy who was going to do the running around for me for a while sat as far forward in the boat as he could get, cross-legged, his dhoti tucked up about his thighs. His long hair was spread out across his shoulders like Miss World; though unlike Miss World he had a beard. He had not moved since we'd started, his eyes fixed on whatever the water happened to bring in front of him. Hari his name was, Haribhai for familiarity. He was a good boy, Martin had said, with functional English, but if you don't understand each other it will have nothing to do with semantics. Like most people, he had said, he's got problems. You'll be doing him more good than he will ever do you. Well, that's what he said.

The two men who did the work, black and thin and

naked but for red rags pulled up between their buns and flapped over the string in front, moved the rough paddles around as if to pull the boat downstream but actually letting the current do all the work. Their backs were dusty, untouched by moisture, while mine was crawling with sweat.

The river, a foetid, dying thing, silting up, slowly bearing down decaying wood and dead plants, released bubbles now and then but not because of the presence of fish. Green scum spread out from stagnant pools into the slow flow of water. Trees, standing on complicated systems of roots, hung down screens of twittering leaves. When we drifted into their shadows it was almost cold, but that was my sickness, not the weather.

I leaned over on one hip and reached for Mickey-Mack. I pulled him out and shook him out and smoothed away his wrinkles and put him on my hand, flicking at the strips of different coloured cloth that were supposed to be his hair.

'Doc,' I said in Mickey-Mack's voice, a nice round choirboy's alto. 'What's Reality?'

Martin played it straight as he always does. After some thought he said: 'It's like a man who's afraid of deep water so he sticks a pole in the river and then lies about its length. It is something to believe in but nothing you can have much faith in.'

'I'm always the straight man,' Mickey-Mack said. Which wasn't true of course. Not if I could help it. I turned Mickey-Mack to me, tapping the inside button to roll his eyes, then tried out his laugh. I do it well, his laugh. He has a kind of frog-like mouth, apple green on the inside, with a foot-long shocking-pink tongue. I flick out the tongue, let go a creaky-door laugh, then snap the mouth shut on the tongue which I then slowly pull back through the fringey lips. I tell you he's a monster. I love him.

'Mike,' said Mickey-Mack. 'I miss Andy Fumbles.'

'Well so do I,' I said. 'But we mustn't fret.'

Andy Fumbles was my other puppet. My first. I think he came with my cradle. He had big long loose teeth you could do funny things with. With Andy Fumbles gone I guess I let Mickey-Mack get away with murder. He went, Andy Fumbles did, when they stole all my things while I was waiting for the ambulance. Mickey-Mack was in my back pocket as usual so they missed him. It was the only thing they did miss.

'Do you think he's gone to Heaven?' said Mickey-Mack.

'Well I should hope so,' I said. 'Though he had a foul temper, and a dirty lip. His mind wasn't so clean either.'

'But he had a nice soul,' Mickey-Mack said.

'Are you sickening for something?' I said.

'I think I am,' he said. 'I could sleep for a week.'

The paddles reached out, guided us through the field of lilies. They were white, almost closed. I reached out to touch a lily pad and it tilted like a green plate and took on a ball of water.

Although the sights and sounds were new, unfamiliar, they were easily taken in: water buffalo, naked boys, storks on mud banks, clouds of waterbirds, long banners of coloured cloth drying on bushes. Unmoved, lethargic, going along with it like it was merely the diversion of a film strip seen many times before.

Martin said: 'Five minutes.'

'Five minutes,' murmured Mickey-Mack. 'What's that mean then?'

'It is a unit of time,' I said.

'Is that so,' said Mickey-Mack. 'A unit of time is it. Measurable, presumably.'

'Indubitably,' I said.

'Always the same is it?'

'More or less.'

'Or faster or slower.'

'Whatever.'

'Or shorter or longer.'

'Okay, okay!'

'Whether from inside the back pocket or outside the back pocket?'

'Well . . .'

'Five minutes! it has a nice round sound but is perhaps without specific meaning?'

'Well, it's easier to measure time than it is to measure people's intelligence, I tell you.'

'Doc, next question: what is time?'

'I have the same problem St Augustine had,' said Martin. 'I know what it is until I try to tell someone about it.'

'St Augustine? Who he?'

'He's the saint who said: "Lord, give me chastity . . . but not yet."'

'Did he now? I can't wait for it to come out on video.'

But his heart wasn't in it so I folded him up, yawning, and put him away. I mean I was yawning when I put him away.

The lethargy was not the result of the brick; Martin had shaved my head and sewed it up like a soccer ball and the scars shone pink and clean through two-week-old bristles. In fact I'd forgotten all about being hit. I held my hand out, moved it in the sun, admired the pretty yellow colour. That had more to do with things than the crack on the head. For in Martin's model hospital they discovered that I had hepatitis, boils, anaemia, dysentery, worms and the habit of saying 'It's kind of a long story.'

The long-story story was mainly a put-off until I had decided what to do. I mean the new passport is no problem, it is just a lot of bother. And money's no problem – I'm loaded, once I've reconnected. It's just that I'm under-age and everything has to go through my guardians. There's two of them. One is Aunty Aggi like Hercule Poirot's friend, though to be honest she lost most of her little grey cells a long time ago. The other is Aunty Mat, as in waltzing, also known as Auntimatter and, when in a disagreeable mode, as The Black Hole. Not that she's disagreeable often. In fact she's okay. But okay in Shropshire. Here she'd be a disaster, calling 'Bearer' all over the place.

Martin, reading my mind like a good doctor, said, 'I still think you should send them a fax.'

'Are you kidding?' I said. 'They don't even have an address. Just a location. If you want to contact them you first draw a picture and then hire special postmen. Japanese.'

'I bet a wire would reach them.'

'They used to have pigeons,' I said. 'But they couldn't find their way home.'

'Surely they'll get worried when they don't hear from you.'

'Listen! When I come home from school they take about three days to work out who I am. There they are, as polite as two penguins, each hoping that the other will introduce us. You know what? They even try feeding me Shredded Wheat in the hope I'll conform. You believe that?'

'The way you tell it makes it hard to believe anything,' he said. 'They still make Shredded Wheat?'

'Theirs might be copies,' I said. 'It smells like peat.'

'They might like it here. Who knows. Though Shredded Wheat never caught on.'

'If they could manage to get their Marmite through security they might be okay. But in the dark ages both of them were nurses in Pune. And the result was serious trauma.'

'You almost sound as if you're not too keen to have them come out and hold your hand.'

'It would be better to let them think I'm still in North Wales. Those foreigners are bad enough. And what would happen to their beagles, for Pete's sake, and their bees, and their pear trees.'

'I somehow get the feeling your aunts and you have rather a contentious relationship.'

'I love 'em. Both. Just believe it,' I said.

But I put Mickey-Mack away too soon, didn't I. A lot of that would have sounded better coming from him. Like he says: I'm tempted to go for laughs even when I know no laughs are there. But you've got to take that risk, haven't you, when you come up against a rational mind.

Martin said that it was the hepatitis which accounted for my current doubts about reality. He said I'd had a bad case of it. He warned me of feelings of depression and fears of going mad. I told him when I felt like that I'd know I was getting back to normal. But he was very gentle with me. I was lucky that his clinic was right round the corner from the riot. But I think he got off the world about the time they discovered where God hid the fuse. I told him when he came with his list of questions that the only trouble with him was that, one: he expected the answers always to be related to the questions, and two: he didn't laugh enough. He said he knew. He said it was the Jesuit in him. But he laughs more than he lets on, which is the opposite of me . . .

Slowly, turning, the river exposed itself, going mainly to one side of a small island on which stood a large house among trees. Beyond it was the sea, seen through coconut palms growing right down to the beach.

Martin nodded. This was it. I couldn't decide whether his eyes crinkled up from the sun or at one of his private jokes.

The house was large, white, sort-of-colonial, secure behind a tall wall which was topped with terracotta tiles. Creepers with orange flowers spilled over the gate and thin palm trees leaned over the wall. A yellow-flowered tree rose like clouds of summer smoke from behind the walls, seeming to fill the courtyard.

But there was something else.

Rising above the tops of the walls, curving out in a fragile dome over the whole courtyard was a fantastic bamboo structure that looked as if it had been built by some mad native genius after a night visit from Buckminster Fuller.

A half-dozen naked men were up on the wall and on the structure tying poles together, on to which bamboo grids were being dropped. One of the men was near the top and every time he moved the structure sagged and leaned and buckled. As we drifted nearer you could hear it creak. An older man who had been shouting up at them with some vehemence from outside the wall turned when he saw us and stood with his hands together at his chest before wading out into the river to wait and hold the boat. Haribhai jumped off over the bow to help him pull it to the bank.

'Trouble with the workers?' Martin said.

'Trouble with my nature,' the man replied.

His skin was very dark. He had thin legs and very big feet. The hair on his chest was white and curling but the hair on his head and chin was clipped short. His ears were long like Buddha's.

'I see you finished in time?' Martin said.

'If we hadn't started at all we'd have been finished in time,' was his answer. My God, I thought, he's Irish.

Martin turned to me and said: 'Om Prakash, this is Michael Flower; he'll be staying a couple of weeks.' The man held his hands to his chest again.

'Namaste,' he said.

I gave him a grin and returned the gesture, still sitting.

Martin jumped on to the bank. 'You haven't lost any?'

'They could have gone any time they wanted to,' he said. His jaw was like a camel's, fitting askew.

They assisted me from the boat as if I were some gimpy old lady. My legs trembled a bit but I was all right. I faced back up the river, looking for reprieve. Here I was, before the age of consent, with no will of my own, recovering from disease, on an unnamed island at the mouth of an unknown river in a country I'd never been to before at a time when I should have been out chasing girls and polishing my flip and learning the words of complaint about the way the world was run. If I had any sense I'd pick up my marbles and go home. If I had any marbles.

The river, before it discoloured the sea, slowly spun in a pattern of whirlpools.

'It's really not much of a river,' I said.

'Just wait a while,' Martin said, looking up at the sky.

'Brag, brag,' I said. It seemed we had known each other a very long time.

The island was like a tear about to be squeezed out into the sea. At the gland end was the house and at the other end was the fringe of trees and the narrow beach. A breeze, which Martin said was constant at this time of year, came down the coast and nipped into the river mouth. The beach was white, and the slow surf where the sun shone through it was saffron.

They got me out without much of a splash and we walked round to the gate which was on the arm of the river that was almost dry.

Old posts had been driven a long time ago into the

river bed two-by-two for a zigzag two-plank walkway but the planks for ten yards had been taken off and so it was unusable as a bridge. The posts were leaning everywhich-way though some men were working on it, straightening them, digging into the sand.

Outside the gate, up against the wall, was a small lean-to shrine with some stone idol clad in a tattered and faded maroon cloth and dabbed in red and yellow dots. Incense smouldered there among some faded flowers.

Haribhai took my arm as if I were rich or feeble-minded and together we made it safely up the steps and through the gate.

The bamboo structure you could see above the wall was not all of it by any means. From the gate to the house was another structure, a covered walkway like the passage into the circus ring from the big-cat cage. Above that, looking crazier than ever from inside, was the virtually fin-ished network of interwoven bamboo, curving up from the walls to the second terrace of the house. It fitted neatly around the palms, covered almost all of the flowering tree, towered over a small mud hut at the end of the garden, chopping up the sun into a mesh of light and shade. The noise I had heard ever since we had approached the island was now explained. Up in the centre of the tree in a hud-dled fury were a couple of dozen monkeys.

'It sounds like an old Tarzan movie,' I said.

Martin didn't look at me as we went down the covered path so I buttoned up. Part of the game we played was to out-cool each other. But here he had the advantage.

At the end of the path was a covered terrace with two

fat columns. The caged passageway opened to it, enclosing a pale green shade set with wicker chairs and a low table and potted plants with white flowers. I slumped down into a squeaking chair. Haribhai quickly moved a stool and lifted my feet on to it. I was soaked with sweat and my mouth tasted as if my tongue had been replaced by a green copper clapper. Martin switched on a ceiling fan which pattered and clanked for a while before settling down into a mechanical whir.

The best I could do was: 'Where's Willie Maugham then?'

Martin moved about, avoiding my eyes, looking up through the inner cage to the larger one, shaking his head, nurturing a small smile.

'I like this,' I finally said. 'At least it's better than Colwyn Bay.' He reached over and took my pulse.

'But I miss my Aunty Mat,' I said, 'with her beef tea.'

We inspected each other for a while, and then he gave in. 'I suppose you'd like to know the whole story. Why I've invited you here.'

'You've already given me enough to get on with.' I said. 'For my health . . .'

'It is cooler, and it's clean. And there's a pretty good cook . . .'

'And to be away from the riots . . .'

'It is quieter. And you need a place until you get your money . . .'

'What's in the small print?'

'I could use your help.'

'Aunty Mat says I volunteer like a Chelsea pensioner but I'm always ready with my cop-out.'

'How else are you going to work off your debt,' he said.

'There's that,' I said.

He turned to the cage, tested its strength. A big male with yellow teeth swung down and yammered at him.

Martin said, 'Om Prakash says he has learned the meaning of thirty-six different monkey sounds.'

'So that's it,' I said. 'You want me to make a rhesus grammar.'

'These are langurs. The holy monkeys. They're unsettled just now because of the cage and the workmen. Usually they are quieter. Better company than a lot of people I know. It's really a very nice place to recover from an illness.'

'It would be a good place to hide from the law,' I said, thinking: if I lost my mind here I'd be crazy for ever with everyone shouting Flower, Flower, looking all over the place, missing me.

'Aren't monkeys flower-eaters?' I asked.

He said: 'I've seen them do it.'

'So then,' I said. 'What's the short way to complete understanding?'

He said: 'There is no short way to complete understanding.'

'You've been in this country too long.'

He said: 'I haven't been here long enough, that's the trouble. That's why I can talk like this, pretending to understand the words I use.'

I gave in. 'Start with the cage.'

'It's a long story,' he said.

'Hey! You're stealing my lines,' I said.

Haribhai came then with two lemonades on a brass tray. The glasses were misted and a sliver of lemon floated in each one. Martin took a sip, placed the glass back on the table, made as if to speak, then looked at his watch, considered something, then got up and held both his hands up, palms out. 'Wait,' he said, and left.

There was nothing really that I wanted and yet I could not say either that I was content. But alone for a moment with only the monkeys for company I was surprised to find that I saw nothing strange about my situation though I couldn't begin to explain my state of mind.

Except for two monkeys who were now slowly and carefully exploring the cage, all the others were still huddled high in the tree. There was a stillness here and yet, within it, constant movement. Plants nodded, grasses moved against each other, palm fronds trembled, small winds rearranged things in the dirt and put in motion swirls of dust. There was a silence that was not offended by the sounds within it: the caws and chirrups, the squeaking and squealing, the knocks and grunts, the secretive rustlings and whisperings. The sound of surf.

The sun came down through the tree in narrow shafts of light, moving about as if to spotlight beetles. A pot of water reflected coins of light on the ceiling.

I closed my eyes, feeling done in. It was the dead time of day with everything – people, dogs, oxen, plants – everything wanting to lie down beneath the weight of the sun. But almost at once a nearby sound made me open my eyes and jerk myself to my feet.

For just inside the cage, naked but for a red string around his little pot belly, was a small child. Unsteady on his feet he looked up and laughed at a large male monkey, hunched in ill temper, who was swinging down from the tree.

'Haribhai,' I called, looking about me.

At my call the child had turned, swayed, and then had collapsed on to the ground. He grinned at me and dribbled, pattering his hands about in the dust.

'Om Prakash,' I yelled, running down the path towards the gate looking for a way in. The monkey, arse-end up, tail curled over his back, walked slowly and stiffly towards the boy.

Then Om Prakash appeared at the gate, questioning. I pointed, too scared and too puffed to do anything else.

He looked into the cage but all he said was, 'Oh, they know each other.'

The monkey, a few feet from the child, stopped and sat, laid out his tail in a curl and examined minutely between his fingers. I held on to the bamboo grille for a moment waiting for the darkness to leave my eyes.

'Listen,' I said. 'I think I don't belong here.'

'Who is saying this?' Om Prakash said.

'Come on now, don't turn Bengali on me,' I said.

The darkness cleared from my eyes in time for me to see a young girl come out of the mud hut. She was something. Soft and full, as plump as those blow-up serpents kids take to the water when they're learning to swim.

'How can you not belong anywhere?' Om Prakash said.

'How?' I said, still watching her. She paused with a brass pot on her hip and gave me a good up-and-down before turning and walking to a covered well.

'I tell you how,' I said. 'You try going to a Cardiff City home match with some limey colours on. That's how for one. You've got to know the rules.'

The pale green of her sari changed colour as she moved into the shade, and the colour of her skin too. Her hair was sleek and reached down in a thick braid which ended in a brass bell. She had bells on her ankles also, silver. Looking at her I guessed I must be getting better.

'The only rule,' Om Prakash said, 'is that you must forget the rules.'

'You sound just like that old man who wrote plays for old men who didn't like plays,' I said.

'Rules are needed,' he said, 'only when you think effect comes after cause.'

'Listen,' I said. 'What you trying to do? Take away all my teddy bears?'

'Nothing causes anything,' he said. 'It just becomes.'

'Oh, becomes,' I said. 'I'm always too slow for the becomes. I consider myself lucky when I can see what was.'

'What was, became, at one time,' he said. 'It is just becoming with the truth extracted.'

'Listen,' I said. 'I've been to everybody about the trouble I have with my ears. As soon as I hear the word Truth everything gets clogged up in there and I get this big buzz.'

'Don't worry about it,' he said. 'Truth is your second nature.'

'I know,' I said. 'But what's my first nature . . .'

My God: had he any idea how much ground we'd covered in this three-minute spot.

The child pushed up with his arms, steadied himself, seemed to consider whether to do a flop on to his back, decided against it, then, pointing his thumbs out ahead of him, he set himself off on his travels. His legs had an arbitrary motion to them, somehow conveying him about but not necessarily where he planned to go. Like he seemed to be heading nornorwest and his feet were taking him nornoreast.

'Don't worry about the boy,' Om Prakash said. 'My wife is never far away.'

I covered my surprise quickly. So all right: he'd got himself a wife who looked like his child, or even his grandchild. Eating my heart out was nothing new.

'That's your boy?' I said, showing my intelligence.

'Yes,' he said, looking as if he too couldn't believe it.

'What's his name?'

'He is called Nataraj.'

'What's that mean?'

'Nataraj was Lord of the Dance,' he said, just as the boy did a spectacular bellyflop into the dust.

'Yes, well,' I said. 'You mustn't be discouraged.'

Om Prakash stayed with me until I got myself collapsed back into my chair then hunkered down near me, his knees up about his ears. His big toes were like kingsize potatoes.

I said: 'Where did you get such big toes?'

He looked down, studied them. 'I was given them on my birthday,' he said.

Soaked with sweat again from my jumping about I sucked at the lemonade like a horse. Om Prakash looked at me in silence for a while then said: 'They are like children these monkeys and have to be watched like children. Seldom dangerous but always in trouble. Inquisitive they are, examining things, carrying them off.' He sounded just like a rural Welshman who had learned English by correspondence, you know, with long waits between lessons.

The workmen appeared at the gate, waggled their heads in question: can we go? Om Prakash waggled his head in reply: you can go. They left and, as if waiting for this signal, half the monkeys gave out great cries and hurled themselves up at the cage, ricocheting around like screaming ping-pong balls. The other half, mothers with young and half-grown animals, scattered just as fast, getting in each other's way, now and then swiping at each other in passing. The cage shook and buckled in their fury.

'Some children,' I said.

Om Prakash got up and, walking slowly, entered the cage through a bamboo gate I had not seen before. Ignoring the commotion he sat down cross-legged under the tree. In the earth near him was set a stone pot with a screw lid. Unscrewing it he put in his hand and brought it out fisted. Immediately a monkey with child came and sat at his feet and he handed her something. Blinking contentedly, with a foot holding on to the tail of her straying child, she nibbled neatly, holding with both hands whatever it was that he had given her. Soon others came down until, except for a few still showing off, it became quieter. One by one they came to him and he handed out their treats, never throwing to them.

I leaned back. Above, the fan creaked round and round. On its hub was painted a red circle and a red dot. Watching it spin it occurred to me that those were the only symbols which when spun did not change their significance . . . 'Here we go,' I mumbled to myself in disgust, closing my eyes. 'Any moment now I'll be planting long poles in the river.'

When Martin came back he looked cool and relaxed and with a shiny look about him.

I said: 'You look as if you've been into the magic gum-drops.'

He did not seem to hear. He sat, sipped his drink, his eyes lidded, his face in repose. I waited, catching a bit of his calm.

Finally he said: 'I'll leave out the Once Upon a Time, shall I?'

'Here we go,' I said. 'Da-da-dah. Disclosure time.' I took a big gulp at my lemonade and dropped my head back, let him have the scene all to himself. But he took his time with it.

'Between the wars,' he finally said, 'there was, I'm sure you know, a very active resistance movement in India. Gandhi was only a part of the picture. There were many men who were dedicated to the overthrow, violent if it had to be, of British rule. One such man planned, so the British said, and he never denied it, the bombing of a railway bridge just at the time a train was due with government officials on it. The bomb went off, like most things in India, late. No one was hurt but they came looking for him and he went into hiding. After some time he came here to this house, but by then something unexpected had happened to him.

'He had found God.

'In India of course there's nothing remarkable in that. There are always, at any given moment, thousands like him – Godmen, saints, mystics, teachers, madmen, fools, charlatans, whatever. But he was something special. And what he was was recognised by the people with whom he settled. The people around here. He became their holy man, loved and venerated.

'The British knew where he was of course but they also knew that he was now different from the man they had earlier set out to find. So they left him alone. And many years passed . . .

'But then there was an administrative change and the new British official decided to settle all the things in his pending file. It was quite an astonishing sight the day the young officer came down to do his duty. You've seen the riots and you've probably got the idea that that is their only reaction to a stress situation. But there are other aspects to their nature.

'Anyway, this evening – a most peculiar day it had been with the monsoon late as now but almost upon us with thunder near and a tremendous tension in the air – this evening down from the barracks came marching this pink and straight young officer with his squad of Indian soldiers. Hup-tup-thrup, looking neither to right or left, down through the village, through the silent crowd that had gathered, come to take away their holy man. Of course he had known about it, was prepared for it, had spoken to them about it, told them how to act.

'Silently the holy man gave himself up, silently he was marched away . . . The day is still celebrated as the day he came back out into the world . . .

'That night a band of sacred monkeys came across the dry arm of the river just before the rains came and took over, as it were, the island. So the villagers disconsolate at losing their holy man accepted instead . . .'

I started to laugh then and it was some time before Martin felt like going on.

'In some ways, it could be said that the villagers here live a charmed life. Cut off by the river and the sea, they are insulated as well as isolated. The climate is reasonably healthy and the water of acceptable standards. Being fisherman they never really know hunger. When they remember, they count their blessings . . . They certainly want nothing changed.

'So then, whenever rain is scarce, whenever this arm of the river gets low, they ask me, as I now own the place, to build a cage for the monkeys to ensure that they remain on the island . . . No more silly really than Churchill and the monkeys of Gibraltar. I always put them off as long as possible and the rains have always come before I needed to do it. Until this year . . . Your head is shaking!'

'Something's loose,' I said.

'They just recognise, you see, the many different

33

aspects . . .' But he did not go on, giving all his attention to his lemon juice, swirling it around in his glass.

Suddenly I felt as high as I ever get. The day seemed to lack nothing. You don't know why and you don't care why. I couldn't think of a single question. I think I even forgot to shake my head. But I couldn't give in that easily. 'Just keep taking your tablets,' I said, but I'm not sure if I said it aloud.

'The house has always had a great peace,' Martin was saying. 'Of course it was different then when I first saw it, with only two rooms habitable and everything tumbling down . . . People here have a talent for letting things fall apart don't you know, rather they have trouble keeping the equilibrium. They are either going up or coming down, rarely staying level . . . When you have lived here as long as I have keeping it in repair is the least you would want to do.'

It was only after a long silence that he went on: 'There's always the danger, I know, that I am merely living out my own myth, a primitive tale if ever there was one symbolising some quite ordinary solar phenomenon or other. But . . . he was real, no myth . . .

'He's not forgotten . . .

'He was that rare holy man, one with a western education: Winchester I believe, and classics at Cambridge. Beautiful Victorian prose. Though the education had little to do with what he was . . .

'Sometimes I imagine him coming across the river with bowling-ball bombs in a doctor's bag, fierce and bearded. I do this only because it is so difficult to remember him as he really was, a much more glorious figure.'

Just for the hell of it, I said: 'Don't you ever miss Battersea Park?'

'You have no idea of the impact he had,' he said, giving my remark the attention it deserved. 'When I first met him – I was about to say, "You know what it's like when you're young," but you are the last one to say that to for all your seventeen years . . .'

He made a gesture to someone over my shoulder. I heard the creaking of bamboo and for a ludicrous moment thought he had conveyed something to one of the monkeys. But it was Om Prakash's wife who came, walking slowly and shyly up the path leading the child who was all over the place, lunging at the limits of her arm, falling over his feet, tipping and wobbling as if his centre of gravity was whirling about inside him. When near to us she gave the palms-together greeting at her throat and the child, freed, staggered up to Martin and clutched his leg. His laughter broke us up. Martin lifted him up and stood him on a corner of the chair and put his arm around him and the child fell against him. With his free hand Martin searched in his trouser pocket and brought out a miniature pink plastic flute into which he blew to produce a cheerful plastic peeble-de-peep. Then he presented it to the boy. Tentatively he put it to his lips, peeped once, twice, three times, then took it from his mouth and let loose a stream of laughter.

Martin introduced us then. Lakshmi she was called.

And we were just trying out a couple of smiles when Haribhai appeared at my side standing very straight, very stiff, waiting until he had everyone's attention. Which didn't take very long.

'When can I see her?' he said.

Martin sighed, looked at me, then at Lakshmi, who looked at Hari seemingly with some disapproval.

'You know what it's like, Hari,' Martin said.

'I need to see her,' Hari said.

After a long pause Martin said: 'I'll see what I can do.'

Haribhai stood for a while as if not wanting to leave it like that, but finally he turned and left.

I waited for Martin to tell me who it was Hari wanted to see but instead he started to talk in Tamil to Lakshmi. Once she glanced my way when presumably something was said about me. She had a vermilion spot between the eyes and a glass and silver flower at one nostril. Ear-studs. Martin must have told her to leave the child with us for, after a moment's hesitation, she turned away. I watched her through the gate. The boy went on laughing and peeping his plastic flute in Martin's ear, while he picked up his train of thought.

'I told you a bit about my wife. She's a zoologist but her interests seldom stay within the confines of her field.

'You'll meet her in a week or so. She's Italian but if it wasn't for her temperament you'd think she was Indian. You'll fall in love with her, of course, as everyone does.' He looked at his watch, stirred, patted the child's belly. The peeping going on.

'She has just been given a grant to investigate a controversial drug in an extra-laboratory situation. The project is in three parts. One is in Japan on the Japanese macaque (Nanda is there now setting it up); one is in Benares on the temple monkeys, the rhesus; and one is here on the langur, the sacred monkey, the hanuman. None of them are what you'd call jungle monkeys . . . There have already been extensive studies on these three groups and we know how they act under normal conditions. But with this particular group we just want to record any changes in habit patterns that this temporary cage might bring about.'

'I don't believe this,' I said. He talked on through my laughter.

'Om Prakash knows more about monkeys than he does about people but Nanda wants it straight on disk, and that he won't do. I thought that perhaps the two of you together could keep a diary of any aberrational behaviour that might occur. A week or two I should think, at most, until the rains. Of course afterwards when we start with the drug you may stay or go as you wish.'

Still laughing I said: 'When you are elliptical I have no trouble believing you, but when you give it to me straight I don't believe a word.'

'Nanda has the same trouble,' he said. 'And she expresses it in almost the same way. But in her language it is ecliptical.'

'What's the drug supposed to do?' I said.

'Better you don't know,' he said. 'That way you won't anticipate its response.'

'You don't know what you're getting,' I said. Three half-grown monkeys who had been chasing each other stopped and looked through the bars as if in sudden astonishment.

Martin called to Hari and stood up, lifting the boy over to me, surprising me so that I fell into that false jolly stuff with him. I joggled him about to make him laugh.

'What's the matter with you then?' I said. 'I've never heard anything but laughter out of you. As the Polish woman said to the butcher, you no got no tongue?' And I squeezed his cheeks, popping open his mouth.

Which wasn't so smart.

The inside of his mouth glistened. Below the little whatyamacallit that hangs down at the back of the throat was a similar little thing at the bottom of the cavern. But no tongue. Martin watched me.

'Yoops!' I said, downplaying it.

Martin said: 'Om Prakash says he will just have to find another way to praise God.'

'What happened?'

'Om Prakash said he came like that.'

'That isn't enough, is it?'

'He says he's welcome no matter what he's missing.'

The boy was laughing up at me, mouth wide as if to display that thing. I laughed back at him but it was no deeper than skin and teeth.

'Introduce him to Mickey-Mack why don't you,' Martin said.

But I shook my head. 'I don't think Mickey-Mack's up to it right now,' I said, handing the boy over to Haribhai.

# 2

## AS THE SUN ON
## STILL WATER

SOME INDIAN SAYS THAT THOUGHTS originate outside the head. How about that. If you want to silence your mind, he says, you merely sit quite still (merely?) and as the thoughts descend and are about to seep into your head you just say nonono and wave them away as if they were wasps about a dish of jam. When I was really sick I tried it. My jamdish was buzzing like summer days and there I was waving away like a boy scout until my arms got tired. But I could see what he meant. I believe him. I'm beginning to believe all kinds of crazy things. Just because you can't do the stuff they say can be done doesn't prove a thing. But can you imagine: big fat balloons of thought hovering over everyone's head, one balloon nudging up against another, sometimes leaking thoughts into the head of someone they're not meant for.

That's what I like about this illness: I can blame anything on it. Right now with the light going and the monkeys setting up what I gather is their usual evening commotion I feel this great trembling inside. And I don't mind it a bit.

The Chinese believe, so Martin tells me, that the liver is where the dreams come from. It makes sense. Illegal substances and drink and diseases of the liver all lift you off the ground. You see things differently when the liver's affected. You remember differently. The past is something you're able to fall away from.

And that's an image I'm right at home with. I never drop out, I fall. I fell out of the womb. 'Untie that thing,' were my first words . . .

Not true of course, then or later. If there was untying done, ever, I don't remember it. In fact, as far as I know, I might still be tied up. All's blank in fact, the first ten years only fragmentary memories of horsing around and complaining and pretending to be hurt and running away from people and swimming in rivers and trying to catch stuff falling from trees frightening birds and chasing cats and sucking icicles. Being silent before immense and funny-smelling ladies. That's about all. I remember less than most people say they do about their previous incarnations. It's as if I were born fully functional at the age of ten. A glimpse here and there, that's all, and then a falling into a ten-year-old's consciousness, with comfortable Aunty Mat and wayward Aunty Aggi there. Ma and Pa if they came back I wouldn't know from two bars of soap.

It was all lovely, then, all falling. Into love and out of it, in and out again. And not only love. All kinds of experiences, and you didn't need to know much either, that's the thing. You didn't even have to believe. You just needed to know how to let yourself go like a kid jumping from a sand-castle into someone's arms. All you had to remember was this:

One: not to feel regret for where you fall from.
Two: down-there is only a place like up-there was.
Three: falling up is as easy as falling down, and the one who is falling is in no position to tell direction.
Four: the moment of falling is one of the few free moments you'll ever know.
Five: falling is only a quick method of covering distance.
Six: the universe is falling. Some say it's falling out, some say it's falling in. Some say there's someone there to catch it, some say no. Whatever they say doesn't matter . . .

But what I'm saying is that somewhere about the time of the second big bang they must have started building us kids differently because no one I grew up with gave much thought to stability or mental health or money in the bank. We don't know where we came from or why we're here; we sure don't know where we're going or if we'll be given enough time to get there. And we don't even wonder much whether they'll let us in if we arrive . . .

You know what little kids are like? They find something on the ground and if they can pick it up they'll stick it somewhere. Up the nose, in the ear, down the pipe. And that's what it's like nowadays with everyone I know. They've tried it. Up the nose, in the ear, down the pipe. And even when they straighten out like me they've been places Aunty Mat and Aunty Aggi never knew existed . . .

What they say – that is the ones who have learned how

to speak – is: don't expect anything from anything. And: if they say it's bad then it's most likely OK. And: the pure in heart is a matter of years. And: knowledge will put you in a cage, experience will set you on your feet. And: doubt, but if in doubt, believe. And: if you start to believe, laugh at it; if it still stands, kneel. And: when you are too old to cry you may be too old to laugh. And: dogma is a signpost put up to give comfort to those not going anywhere . . .

In a few days I'll be eighteen. Then, presumably, as now, I'll be five feet eleven, a temporary one-twenty-five. I'll have black hair I'll have to call short for a while, a wispy attempt at a Fu Manchu, a slight limp, an extra bone in each ankle, a crooked nose, blue eyes set in greeny whites. I will, I suppose, still be addicted to skin diving, peanut butter on a spoon, birds, and birds, more birds, moving about, anything you can plug in or switch on . . . Flower, Flower, that's me, open at dawn, closed at dusk. Dies in winter, comes up in spring . . . 'Flower,' a sweet young twit once said to me, checking out my ID, 'is merely the word for the reproductive organs.' I liked that. She loved figures of speech, that girl did. 'The female part of the flower contains the stigma,' she'd say. 'The male has the stamina.' She also liked to put on me all kinds of archaic stuff, like: 'The dandelion is the lion's tooth; the daisy is the day's eye . . .'

Daisies are larger in India . . . Larger, sweeter, realer, lovelier . . . I think I'm really losing all my buttons, you know? I'm loving too many people. I'm loving too many things. As I said: I even love my puppet . . .

Remember that old movie about a ventriloquist who

started to live his life through his dummies? He ended up in a wet sheet. But you know, you can really get involved. The lines are spoken, gestures are made, you work the eyeballs from inside the head and before long you feel that there are knobs and levers in your head too, and that someone is working you just as you are working them. The two things going on simultaneously. I want to smile when they smile, I pull a long one when they do . . .

Once, in the hospital, I had this dream where I was in a puppet factory and they were all in rows, still, mute, smiling their painted smiles. Suddenly they were some-how activated and they began to riot, throwing things, screaming, murderous . . .

Like Indians. Mostly passive, submissive, slow to rouse, moved usually by something deep inside. Then suddenly, on some strange say-so – w-w-w-watch out! . . .

That's what it felt like in Madras. One bunch in one street listening to one guy, another bunch in another street listening to another; one guy with one complaint, the other guy with another. Everything seemed OK until the responses became cadenced, rhythmical, urgent. One crowd streamed towards the American consulate, the other heading for the university; at the Chief Minister's palace they met and mingled. And BOOM! I was a puppet caught in a puppet riot.

'Hari!' I called sleepily.

He looked up, trying to anticipate my words. But he didn't have a hope.

'You be careful,' I said, 'you don't pay tribute to any false puppets.'

'Once there was a company of fools stopped on the banks of a river.' Om Prakash, naked but for the strip of cloth around his loins, standing thigh-deep in the river, paused in washing himself and looked down at the water swirling about him in the gathering dusk.

'The first fool said: what a waste of water, all just going into the sea.

'The second fool said: it flows so slowly it will never reach the sea.

'The third fool said: it would never be noticed by the sea even if it reached there.

'The fourth fool said: no, the sea is filling up. Soon there will be no room for any more water.

'And the chief fool said: if we could find the river's source we could dam it up so that the sea would never overflow . . .'

Om Prakash went back to his washing, cupping water in his hands, pouring it again and again over his shoulders, the water sparkling in the last of the light.

'And that is what they tried to do. But, easy as it seemed, they could not find the source. In fact they even lost the river. Finally they settled on a village pump which they polished and put their names on.'

These days all my mots were coming so slow that by the time I thought of them they weren't so bon any more. When I finally thought of something to say it was much too late so I let it go.

It had been a strange afternoon with people coming and going and with sleep coming and going, and then everyone eating separately and at different times, companionable but not in touch. And now it was a strange evening, calm, with bats fluttering low and palm trees standing out against the sky like a row of Japanese helmets. Across the wide part of the river, on the high bank, people were gathered, sitting down, facing out towards the sea, east, the sun already set in the hills behind them. From the nearby bank, across the dry arm, people had been coming and going for an hour or so by way of the zigzag series of planks that had now been repaired and completed, coming to the shrine outside the gate. They performed their acts, knelt or prostrated themselves, dib-dabbed, did circles in the air with their sticks of incense, sat for a while, left. It had taken up the time of dusk, this ritual, had ceased with darkness. There was still the smell of incense and the tiny points of fire but the light was now too dim to see the smoke.

A small wind nosed up the inlet, into the grasses at the river's edge. The water buffaloes that had stood nose-deep in the water now lumbered up the river bank as dark shapes and disappeared among the trees. Distantly a Catholic bell, closer the hushing of the sea, nearby the splashing of water. Towards the north dark clouds gathered, lightning playing silently within them.

Om Prakash came out of the river, his body gleaming as if from oil, the hair on his chest in tight white curls. He moved his hands down his body and his limbs, getting rid of some of the water. Then he stood very still.

'Move yourself to this flat rock,' he said. 'A pambu wants to come and drink.'

Cool as you like but a bit briskly I moved over to the

rock he indicated and sat down, looking about me. I'd
never heard the word before but I knew what he was talking about. After a while I saw its shape, dark and sinuous,
moving among the stones. Near the water's edge it dipped
down, most of it hidden in the reeds. The only way to be
cool with Om Prakash, I was finding out, was to maintain
silence. Little word games with him never scored a point.
Still wet, he draped the cloth around his waist holding the
ends with arms wide, then, bringing the ends quickly
together in front, he folded and tucked them in so that he
was neatly covered to his ankles, his chest bare. For a
moment he stood quite still, then sat, his legs tucked
under him.

We were all facing the sea, the people on both banks,
Om Prakash and I. The wind dropped, the river made
little noise, the Catholic bell finished its business. The
birds had stopped and long ago the monkeys. Now only
the small sound of the sea with long pauses in between
the waves, like very relaxed breathing.

When I swallowed I was afraid I'd disturb the congregation and they'd turn on me like a man with hiccups at
High Mass.

I guess that's why I finally broke it, ashamed a bit to do
it but not being able to stop it, part of me eager enough to
break it.

'What is the business,' I said, 'of sitting all knotted up
like a pretzel?' I was hoping he'd say: what's a pretzel? But
of course he didn't. He acted as if he had them all the time
with his evening beer.

But it took quite some time after he had settled himself before he answered.

'First you stop your body from moving,' he said, 'and then you stop your mind from moving.'

'What you want to do that for then?' I said.

'I will give you the conventional answer,' he said. 'Think of a pond over which blows the wind. The images reflected there are broken up, unclear. But if the wind should cease the surface would become still. And what should we see then reflected there? Shouldn't we see reflected there the world as it is, un-fragmented?'

I sat still for a bit with him.

'You mean,' I said finally, 'this isn't the way the world is?' Which, when you think of it, is not a very bright way to put it. Anyway he didn't answer. So after a while I thought I'd lead him on. 'It's true from here you wouldn't know your country was in riot.'

'Riot!' he exclaimed. 'I am in turmoil. You are in turmoil. You'd expect my country not to be in turmoil?'

'What to do?' I said, trying out the accent.

'When there is riot enough to interrupt the rising of the moon,' he said, 'then we shall have something to worry about.' He made a noise like: woosh! 'One settles for agitation when one cannot attain peace.'

'I had a girl once who, every time I got clever, would say: define your terms.'

'Agitation is trying to be everywhere at the same time. Peace is achieving this.'

'Is that your own?'

'Nothing is my own,' he said. 'We are all like that company of fools, not understanding. All is love running endlessly into love.'

He waited so long I thought he had fallen off into trance. But then he spoke.

'Once a famous builder of cities was approached by an old lady who said: "God is coming on the 28th of February in such-and-such a year, at such-and-such a place. I want you to build me a city for Him." The builder said: "You are mad." And the old lady said: "Here is the money." So he built her a city. What a city! Pools and flowers and spires and spaces. New and open, grave and joyous. And it was finished by the date she specified, the 28th of February of that year, in that place. And along with the old lady and the famous builder of cities thousands of people went up to the top of the hill in the centre of the city and looked down upon all that had been built with love, and the skill and the consciousness that love can bring. And . . . what do you think happened?'

In the dark I shook my head, as if he could see.

'God came down.'

There was silence then, for what can you say to something like that.

The moon when it appeared was like the first of a thousand eyes. In a while I knew they would all appear, at random, each set on a different course, climbing into the night but not illuminating the sky or casting light upon the earth, merely dazzling on the water. O Michael Flower, Michael Flower, you are losing all your petals boy, your little seed pods are starting to rattle.

'You are all masters of fiction,' I said. 'You know that?'

He did not answer and time must have passed. Alone with my thoughts I was not aware that we had lapsed into silence until a nightbird called and drew me back from where I'd been.

I looked across at Om Prakash. His back was very straight, his head balanced with his nose slightly pointing down, his legs tight-crossed and his hands resting palms up on his thighs. I got up. He did not move. Quietly I moved away, thinking of snakes and silence, not wanting very much to go back into that ancient and creaking house but not much wanting either to press my luck.

Just inside the gate I jumped six feet. A dark figure stood there, blocking my way. Then I saw it was Hari.

'Cripes!' I said.

'This is a holy place,' he said in a kind of stern whisper.

'Yes,' I said.

'We all must be holy in it.'

'Yes,' I said. Which shows you, doesn't it, that I had all my switches on.

Finally he stepped aside, and as I passed him he started out to where Om Prakash sat by the barely moving river.

The moon shone obliquely over the wall, down through the cage. The walls of the house were silver, the open windows dark tunnels. Half-way up the path I passed under the faint whispering of the tree. There was the ticking of some insect, the craacking of a frog. No sound from the sleeping family of sacred monkeys. The house was still. How strange silence is. By existing, it can destroy everything man-made if you enter deeply enough into it.

Can destroy everything. Everything we respect and hold dear. Everything that passes away.

Then a woman began to sing. A young voice. Somewhere near. A strange song. Soft, repetitious. Over and over and over, the same phrase. Gentle, full of peace . . . Om Prakash's wife, I thought, until I saw that she sat, silent, in the doorway of her hut . . .

I awoke briefly in the night with the moon a silver trapdoor on my floor and a silver window on my mosquito net. It was very still. A warm wet air was on my face as if something was breathing on me. 'Hey listen!' I said, aloud I think. 'Go away. Hear? There's nothing here for you but me and I'm not ready to go yet.' But it wasn't ghosts, nothing dead and bad but something alive and maybe good. And I was afraid of it.

# 3

# NOTHING PLUS NOTHING EQUALS EVERYTHING

I AWOKE WITH ORDERS ECHOING in my head: double sentries, dig deep, stay alert, watch out. We'd had a hell of a scare and we nearly got took. I don't know what it was all about but I almost got suckered into something. All I really knew was that I was glad of the day with its sunlight and smell of roses, and the rattle of teacups.

Hari, seen through the mosquito net, was waiting with the tray. It was arranged pretty but it was the same old stuff: tea with lemon, dry toast with jam, curd with honey, orange pill. But with a different house maybe there'd be a different jam.

'Good morning M-Mum-Michael,' Hari said. It had been some job trying to convince him of the correctness of the greeting and he was hesitant still. 'Breakfast.'

He put down the tray and hooked up my net. I gave him a sly dekko but in the daylight he was a different man altogether. No stern guardian, no prophety whispers, no threat at all really.

The sun was the other side of the house and all the light was reflected. It was a pretty room, big with enough beds for a harem, downstairs and facing the back garden which was outside the zoological enclosure. Against the outside wall rose bushes had been trained to climb, branches splayed and pinioned. Pink they were, the roses. Before them was a line of palm trees, wrist-thick, house-high.

The window shutters were open and Hari now opened the ten-foot doors. Beyond the terrace, down two steps, was a kitchen garden. Crows conversed in an unfriendly manner on the top of the wall.

While I ate (same jam, yellow, could be anything), Hari sat on the terrace, cross-legged. He had been bringing me meals for a week and had got into the habit of waiting, back decorously turned, in case there was anything I needed. There never was.

I was crunching on my last toast when Om Prakash came into the garden. Hari got to his feet and put his hands to his chest in greeting. But Om Prakash, seeming not to see him, went straightway to work turning over the earth with a hoe-like thing a foot long.

Then occurred something out of Charlie Chaps. In India, as a sign of veneration to old people, parents, sages, etcetera, one bends down and touches their feet. This apparently Hari now decided to do to Om Prakash. He had done nothing like it when we came yesterday, in fact he had ignored him, but apparently things had somehow changed and now he was tippy-toeing down to where Om Prakash was working. He stood around awkwardly until he thought he had a chance and then dived down for the touch. Om Prakash, almost spastically, as if he had spied a scorpion just where he was going to put his foot, danced away, for a moment both feet wide and off the ground at the same time. Hari missed and dabbed at the earth. Om Prakash stared in a kind of angry amazement for a moment then went furiously to work with his hoe, chopping about at Hari's feet, making him back off. He stood there, his face blank, hands to his chest and head bowed. Still working away Om Prakash said something to him so that he turned and came back to the terrace outside my room.

'What was that about?' I asked when I was sure there was no laughter in my voice.

But Hari just bent for my tray and took it away.

I went then into the bathroom next door and sat on a stool under the shower head and turned on the tap. The room was high and large and echoing, the window also opening on to the kitchen garden. At the sound of the splashing water Om Prakash looked up and waggled his head at me in greeting. It was a very public bathroom.

I turned off the tap while I soaped myself. 'I enjoyed your dance,' I said.

'That boy!'

'You ought to be able to stand a little worship now and then.'

'He's like a pot with many mouths – you never know what he's going to open up for.'

I turned on the water again and let it run over me for a while, doing very little work. Over the sound of the water I heard Hari come back into my room. Om Prakash started to turn back to his work so I spoke, just to keep him there.

'That's a nice garden.'

'A gentleman taught me,' he said. 'He was from foreign and showed me everything. Roses up-tight, straight rows, manure-water, stakes with labels.' He turned away and I let him go.

Roses up-tight! That just about made my day. When I had dried myself off and had gone back into my room Hari was looking disapprovingly at himself in the full-length mirror.

'Nothing you can do about it now,' I said, 'except keep it clean and tidy and free from lumps.'

'I could just as well be selling stamps,' he said, fingering his long hair.

'You could at that,' I said. He couldn't though – not with those poppy eyes.

'You should never expect to be safe,' he said, 'serving the Lord.'

'Hey, pick on someone your own weight,' I said.

'Can I go to the village for half-hour certain?'

I said OK, that I didn't need him. And he leaves me. I put on a pair of whites and zip them up and – zap! That's it. Clad.

'Om Prakash!'

He looked up.

'Come and sit in the cage with me and talk monkeys,' I said. 'While I adjust to the day.'

He looked briefly up at the sun as we do at a watch, then put down his hoe and followed me, stopping only to take up a knot of cane and a chair with a broken seat.

In the front the sun was caught, flashing, in the tree as

the branches moved before it. Om Prakash's wife was sweeping inside the cage, the twigs of the short broom marking the dust like in a Japanese sand garden. The monkeys were moving about, munching on leaves it looked like, but listless and quiet except for the half-grown ones who made fitful gestures at each other. Already it was warm and the courtyard was rich with life, birds everywhere and squirrels, sand-coloured lizards trying to climb everything, butterflies air-dancing, enormous bumbling beetles flying into walls, dragonflies pairing off in flight. Flies beginning their lower devotionals, ants their everyday commerce.

I put on the Willy-Maugham and sat under it in the same place as yesterday, listening to the same creak. Seeing us, Om Prakash's boy, naked as before, started to come over.

Om Prakash squatted nearby, his back to the cage. From the folds of his dhoti he brought out a pair of steel-rims and hooked them carefully over his ears and peered through the glass with some sense of accomplishment.

'You look like my Aunty Aggi,' I said. 'She has a special pair of bible specs for church.'

'I have no trouble seeing the Divine,' he said, 'but I can't tell my rice from my fingers.'

He started to hook the cane through the bottom of the chair.

'I thought in India,' I said, admiring his dexterity, 'everyone did just the one thing, like in a union, and caste forbade you to do the thing other than that which you did.' My God! I was even beginning to speak like them. 'I mean there's one for blowing the nose, another for wiping the eyes, another for the matchstick in the ear.'

'It is partly the roses gentleman,' he said. 'He taught me to try many things. And it is partly that I must have had an unpromising horoscope for I was abandoned at birth. A sonless Brahmin took me in and so I never knew what caste I was. I am rare, for I am flexible.'

The boy gurgled at us through the bamboo.

A couple of sparrows came flashing down from the outside world, down through the outer cage, through the inner cage, to perch sideways on the stalks of some potted plants.

'Tell me,' I said, getting to work, not believing any of it, but doing my first stroke. 'Has the cage made any difference to their behaviour?'

'Would it, do you think, to yours?'

I could see he was going to make me sweat for it.

'Sure,' I said, looking about me. 'But it would take someone else to say how.'

'It has made a difference.' Then he made a little speech in a rather formal manner, using mannerisms I hadn't seen him use before but not putting on an act; it was as if he had a teacher he admired and when the occasion merited formal speech he automatically used his teacher's gestures and his inflections of speech.

'If the cage was not there,' he said, 'and they were con-gre-gated in the tree and you walked below them they would not bother much beyond making a few nervous sounds, for their territ-ory would remain bordered by some insig-nificant twig, some patch of indef-inable air.

You en-croach on the ground and they would push out the boundary in the air. But now things are different. The lim-its of their territ-ory are clearly defined in the air as well as on the ground. Walk through the inner cage now, and if they did not know you, they would riot.'

He paused, his jaw askew, a bit surprised at what had come out. Then, 'Notice how many cling to the outside bamboo.'

I counted. 'Six.'

'Yesterday at one time there were thirteen. Tomorrow or the day after there will be none. Then if you bring in the walls of the cage they will not bother much any more, accepting it all until they are confined into a tiny quarter, unclean, unpro-ductive, uncaring.'

'Have they always lived here?'

'They move. Each day a little, changing their bound-aries. From this place to that place, down to the sea, back to this place. Sometimes in this tree if there were no visitors.'

'Then you had to chase them in?'

'A three-day job. There is an old bachelor monkey who follows the tribe but for some social vio-lation he is not permitted to join it. As long as he stays his distance they toler-ate him, but if he gets too close they become agit-ated. The men who rounded them up were always trying to put him in with the others, and as soon as that hap-pened everyone else got out.'

'Where is he now?'

'The bachelor? Where the others should be, roaming about on the island, getting his own fruit.'

'Poor beggar,' I said.

'Perhaps. But it is like that with all of us except that the ones outside the tribe outnumber those within.'

That didn't seem right but where do you go to check it out. I let it go. But I finally traced down a thought that had been wandering around for a long time.

'You know what I feel about a cage?' I said. 'I feel that others can see in more than I can see out.'

Three monkeys came down to where the boy was shaking the trellis. Their black bodies were glossy, their brown heads yellowish in the sun. They were the same size as the boy but with tails longer than their bodies.

'Invite him in,' I said. 'Or out as the case may be . . . The one without the tail.'

He got up and let his son through the wicket gate, the other three standing on their knuckles and grinning. His son staggered along the side of the cage and stood, swaying as if to some inner whacky music, near his dad. I called him over but he wouldn't come until I woke up Mickey-Mack.

Om Prakash took off his glasses and stared at him. It's funny how you can separate your audience. All children to a certain age will look at the puppet and never at the manipulator. Older people tend to look most of the time at the manipulator. Om Prakash looked only at the puppet.

'Well, Hel-lo there,' said Mickey-Mack. Nataraj immediately came over and put his elbows on my knee, his face so close to Mickey-Mack his eyes crossed.

'Er . . . vannakum,' said Mickey-Mack. Then he turned to me. 'Now what. That's all the Tamil I know.'

'Listen,' I said. 'He can't understand you, but he can't misunderstand you either. Tell him a story why don't you.'

'OK,' said Mickey-Mack. 'Once-upon-a-time. There was a group of woozy poobles who lived down by the pillow gastrie under a wiggle strop . . .'

The boy let out a peal of laughter.

'You're right,' Mickey-Mack said, laughing back at Nataraj with his tongue fully extended. 'Slurp!' he went, pulling it back in.

'But one day the head pooble, who had more than once gravelled all by himself, entirely exclapulated all over the shop, sending towers of flimsey strudles . . . three . . . miles . . . down . . . the . . . road.'

He puts his hands over his eyes. 'I don't think I can keep this up,' he said.

'Why not?'

'I'm acting. How come you're having me acting?'

'Sometimes you manage these things better than I do.'

'I don't think I can go on.'

'Sure you can,' I said. 'Make an effort.'

His lips began flapping but no sound came from them. 'You know what I like about you,' he finally said. 'You let me speak to myself now and then, but I don't pay much attention because, to be honest, the chance is pretty good that I've heard it all before.'

'Are you beginning to get mad at me?'

'You do put me, sometimes, in awkward situations.'

'Only when with people who don't understand what you are saying.'

He thought a bit then tapped a floppy finger on

Nataraj's cheek. 'And you know what I like about you? You are incomplete, that's what you are.'

I glanced at Om Prakash in case an apology was in order. But it seemed not to be expected.

'Or . . . not yet ready . . .'

I let him flounder.

'But if you were in my profession you wouldn't be much use no matter who had you on their stupid fist . . .'

Then, of all things, he let out his tongue. Way out, till it reached what would be his collarbone if he had a collarbone. Nataraj went to grab it but Mickey-Mack pulled it back in.

'There it is, gone,' he said, going 'Heh! Heh! Heh!'

And they played awhile, tongue going and coming and Nataraj laughing and trying to catch it and Mickey-Mack going, 'Heh! Heh! Heh!'

Mickey-Mack slowed down and gaped, looking towards the garden gate. 'Well what d'you know!' he said, letting his mouth hang wide open. We turned to see what he saw.

It was Hari. But not the Hari we knew. Hari different. Hari in uniform. He had discarded his shirt and was wearing his lower cloth tied up as some kind of designer bloomers rather than letting it hang straight to his ankles. Round his neck he wore huge prayer beads made from walnutty seeds. On his forehead was the ashy imprint of three fingers. And his head was shaven, and his beard was gone.

Om Prakash, all trace of formal manner gone, said to me: 'The next thing you know he'll be sky-clad.'

Hari, eyes down, said: 'I had lice.'

'You want to start this thing with a dirty mouth?' Om Prakash said.

'It is true,' Hari said. 'I had lice.'

'Do you think you are so special you shouldn't now and then have lice?'

'You shave your head,' Hari said.

Om Prakash scrabbled at his bristled scalp.

'You were even a sannyasi?' Hari said.

'Who told you such nonsense?' Om Prakash said.

'The hair-cutter.'

'Hair-cutter! Don't you know it is the hair-cutter's job to let a little blood and spread a little gossip. Your job is to look after Mister Michael, not sit about listening to the cutter of hair-chatters.'

'I will look after.'

'Leisure is the first thing for you to renounce,' Om Prakash said. 'Quick, bring something for Mister Michael, cool and sweet.'

'I will bring,' said the unhappy Hari.

'Then go back to village. Find bamboo shop. Ask for Subramani. Say he must change cage.' His eloquence seemed to have left him. 'Say big wind coming and bamboo pieces all tied to tree. What kind job is that. Tree moving, bamboo not. All broken.'

'I will go,' said Hari, head down.

When Hari had left I said, 'I've always wanted to get my hair chat by a good hair-chatter.' Om Prakash went back to work on his chair bottom. 'Why you so mean?'

'Mean? I'm not mean.'

'Well they couldn't call you encouraging.'

'Some have to be coaxed; some have to be bullied,' he said. 'Some have to be tricked, and some you must try to dissuade.'

'For what purpose?' I said.

'What for what purpose?' he said. 'For any purpose.'

'What set him off?' I said.

'It could have been anything. Clearly he has been considering it for long. He is the age for it, that's all. With boys like him it is to be expected.'

'So what will he do?'

'Do? How do I know? He may fall in love and let his hair grow again and wear wide trousers. He may become a silly assistant in some temple, carrying about coconuts and yellow flowers, oiling the idols. He may go on the road and find life too hard and the way of the Lord obscure and come back and plant rice. Or, going that way, he may find God.'

'Is that the way to find God?'

'Why not? Sannyasis find God also.'

He briskly picked up the broken chair and the cane. 'Let him try,' he said. 'He may find him if he gets enough wisdom not to ask anyone where to look. He must certainly overcome the in-clination to ask me.'

'He could do worse,' said Mickey-Mack, whom we had all forgotten. 'He could ask him,' nodding at me.

Om Prakash wagged a bunch of cane in the air. 'As long as it's not me,' he said.

Om Prakash's wife came then to the wicket gate carrying a brass tray with something on it covered with a cloth. A thermos bottle was slung over her shoulder like a bandolier. Opening the gate she paused for a moment with her hip thrown forward and her head bent down so that her flower-tucked braids swung free. When she was through the gate she closed it with her plump bottom.

Inclining her head to Om Prakash and nodding towards the house she went on inside and up the stairs. Hari came, eyes down, and placed a lemonade at my side. Then at a gesture from Om Prakash he picked up Nataraj and took him away, though he made a bit of fuss over wanting to take Mickey-Mack with him.

'We didn't talk much about your monkeys,' I said.

'My monkeys!' he snorted, starting to walk away. 'They are probably calling me their man.'

'Is there really a big wind coming?'

'Yes,' he said over his shoulder. 'Bringing with it rain.' And was gone.

The clouds showed no sign of rain to me. They were towering and travelling fast but white and peaceful-looking, full only, it seemed, with the shining of the sun.


When I started to explore the house the first room I came to upstairs was the library but I put that off till later as it was at the top of the first floor stairs and I could check that out on the way down. The first floor was tiled in black and white diagonal squares just like the ground floor, cool and echoing.

All the rooms were high-ceilinged, blue-raftered, the whitewash on the walls flaking like a proper bistro. Except for the rooms facing the front where the monkeys could get in, all the shutters and the doors were open. Taller than me, they were, even if I had my arms up and was standing on a box. Small niches had been worked high up in the walls, all with little stone figures in them. It was still and dark and musty. Also a bit creepy. Not cobwebby creepy, for everything was clean and orderly, and the pieces of furniture – chests and tall cupboards – few, but there was that kind of dark watchful stillness that takes some getting used to.

The library was a corner room. Next to it were two adjoining rooms with everything open; books and papers scattered in what was clearly Martin's, neatly shelved and piled in Nanda's. Both of them contained all the paraphernalia of modern man: laptops, CD players, cameras, airline bags. Lots of colour and plastic. In Martin's room the only things of some age were two yellowed photographs in silver frames set on a window table with a shallow crystal bowl before them in which floated small white flowers. One of the photographs was of a dark, brigandy type of Indian with fierce eyes and upside-down handlebars. The other was of a woman, also Indian, much younger, light-skinned, with a lovely smile, big and open. She wore a sari but a bit casual around the boobs and not pulled over her head, and she stood with her legs apart, one in front of the other. It had a bit of hilltop feeling to it, the smile conveyed outwards to the elements.

Behind the library, at the back of the house, was a verandah and a second staircase open to the outside. This I took, seeing more of the countryside as I climbed, seeing over the wall with the roses, across the slow-moving river to the rice-paddies and banana plantations beyond, and also, the other way, over the drying arm of the river to the beginnings of the village. With clouds turning over, the sky had acquired plenty of shape. Birds were everywhere: swallows or swifts or something low about the tops of trees, pigeons clattering over the village, green parrots – fifty? hundred? – flipping out over some berries on a tree, kites – the bird kind – sailing round and round on the high thermals.

At the top of the stairs, letting my knees stop their shimmying, looking down at the view, I found myself holding my breath. What came into my mind was this: the cessation of noise is the most reliable of warnings that animals use to convey danger to another member of the species. For no known reason I felt my scalp crawl.

Slowly I turned and looked down the passageway. On this floor too all the doors were open except the one into the far room.

Two steps inside, away from the verandah, was like stepping through some kind of sound baffle that cut out all the everyday noises of the world, reducing you, as you passed, to perplexity. Not that the silence inside the house was the absence of noise either. It even had a substance, a rhythm. It was not silence even; rather it was a quietness in which you were waiting for something to come from somewhere beyond the limits of the senses.

What a load of stuff! I wasn't scared, don't get me wrong; I just felt out of my depth, unprepared. In a word: lost. But not the nightmarish feeling of looking for a way where no way seems to be, but a feeling of waiting for someone to lead you somewhere when you are not sure whether that someone is really there or not. I've felt it before, but not often. Usually at those times I bring out Mickey-Mack and as he depends on me I have to pull myself together and act dependable. Noel-Coward-like, you know. Is that his name? Late show on telly? Handsome, sure of himself, hundred grams of plums in each chop? Rude as hell. His type's gone for good.

Then I thought I heard Martin's voice. Very quiet from behind the one closed door. I went up to it and listened. No nonsense. Up there like the butler with the licence to do it. But it was all silent again. Any moment now I felt he'd open up and there I'd be standing with egg on my face.

There it was again.

'Harm?' Or it might have been Charm. Or Calm. Just the one word.

More silence.

'Could there be danger?' It was Martin all right.

A longer silence.

Then again came his voice. 'It is difficult sometimes to do what is important because of the things that are urgent.'

It was definitely Martin's voice but it was a Martin I'd never met. It was a Martin without any Martin in it. You know what I mean?

I backed off, suddenly in a hurry, not wanting now to be caught there. I was down the stairs on bendy knees, like Wyle E. Coyote, holding my breath, with only a glance through the open door of the room at the end of the hall. At the library I nipped in and plopped into the chair set at the table.

Forget it I said. Forget it. Roocoo, roocoo, came the answer from outside the side window. Roocoo is about right; but cuckoo would be better, I thought. But forget it. And I did my best, looking around . . . It was not a big room, the library, and there weren't that many books. Six bookcases maybe, each a bit taller than me, but this was all pre-paperback stuff and most of them were fat. No novels. No poetry after Donne, except for Blake. No 'about' books. And all texts in, it seemed to me, the original languages: English of course, French, German, Greek, Latin – Hebrew maybe? And Indian languages. Philosophy, yoga, I guess. Not much there for me.

The dark table was so polished you could shave in it. Nothing on it except a silver candlestick and some notebooks with leather spines and corners. I flicked through the pages: they were written in Italian so I guessed they were Nanda's. Brilliant! At first I thought they were written only on the right-hand page but then I saw that on some of the left-hand pages were written, mostly in English, sundry quotations about monkeys.

Things like: what pretty things men will make for money, quoth the old woman, when she first saw a monkey.

And: when they are young monkeys are very friendly, but they soon learn.

And: no monkey ever laughs at another.

And: the higher up the monkey climbs, the more he shows his tail.

And: the question is not can they reason? Not can they talk? But can they suffer?

And: man, like the monkey, ceases to be amusing outside his cage.

And: a monkey on the back calls for cold turkey up front.

And: the only reason monkeys don't talk is that they're afraid they'll be put to work.

And: in bush cuisine monkeys are roasted over hot coals on a spit. But the head is chopped off first as it tends to unsettle the guests.

And: man is God's ape.

And: to catch a monkey construct a cage, without a means of entry, around a banana. The bars should be so close together that a hand with fingers extended can be inserted but closed around the banana cannot be pulled back through.

And: if you catch a monkey and dress it up in a new coat only the hill-monkeys will bow to it.

And: at twenty men are peacocks; at forty, lions; at sixty, serpents; at eighty, monkeys and at ninety . . . worms.

And: monkey see, monkey do.

And: time will come when people will disclaim kinship with us as we disclaim kinship with monkeys.

And: in India, the monkey is known not only for his curiosity but also for his devotion.

And: the monkey expresses vigilance, the presence of the whole being and the capacity for seeing all the movements of the consciousness.

And: you ask of the way. There is the way of the kitten with its mother, all trust and surrender; and there is the way of the young monkey, the clinging, all self-effort.

And: O nobly born, there will dawn from the east . . . the blue monkey-headed goddess of inquisitiveness, holding a wheel . . . Fear not that.

Well, maybe. But you can see the different ways, can't you, the East and the West approach things. As Martin once said, the West is not interested in wisdom, but knowledge, perhaps not even knowledge, but theory . . .

But what was he up to up there, speaking so soft, and to whom, or to what? And why was he not getting any answers?

I thought quite a bit, as I do in times of great perturbation, before bringing out you-know-who. For I don't want to seem a kook. Usually I bring him out only when there's others about. I mean it would seem odd wouldn't it, having these conversations with just him and me. Normally I only bring him into a discussion when I think he has something to contribute, or when I want to insult someone, or when I don't want to take sides, or when I want to hear a particular joke for my own entertainment, or when I want to be provocative, or when I want something said I'm too ashamed to say myself, or . . . well for any other reason, really, that occurs at the moment of impulse.

But occasionally, now and then, when the need arises, at moments of stress, when nothing else offers itself, I am known to let him emerge when no one is in earshot. In whispers, mind you. We talk then. Nothing flagrant.

Anyhow finally I brought him out, brushed him down.

'Ooh,' he went, looking round. 'Nice. I could really work on my vocabulary here.'

'And pick up some foreign phrases too,' I said. 'But lower your voice.'

'Andy Fumbles would have loved it. All this light. And not a cobweb in sight.'

'Cobweb? Are you being esoteric?'

'He didn't like spiders, Andy didn't.'

'Who does,' I said.

'Show me round why don't you,' he said.

So I got up and I did my bit, and he looked, bending and stretching to look at the titles and going 'Well I never' and 'H'm, H'm.' The bookcases had glass doors and each one had fat but new-looking brass keys.

'How do you know if they are in English or not,' he said. 'I can't read any of the titles.'

I opened a case. The smell of old paper came out.

'Pooh!' he went.

'That's the smell literature makes when you forget about it for a while,' I said.

I took a book out, thick and heavy, and put it down on a shelf that was only partly filled, and opened it. It was Greek. The margins were covered in tiny, neat handwriting, the ink brown with age.

A silverfish made a dash across the page for the safety of the spine.

'Bzz, bzz, bzz,' said Mickey-Mack, his head wagging back and forth as if he were reading. 'Very interesting. Next.'

I closed the book and put it back in place, closed the door and locked it.

Mickey-Mack looked round, said 'Oh,' and pointed. On

top of the next bookcase sat three frogs almost shoulder to shoulder. I lifted him up to have a good look. They didn't move an eyeball; just throbbed their throats at him.

'Hello froggies,' he said. 'Waiting for the shops to open?'

I shook him to remind him he was in a library, and put a finger to my lips.

'What kind of shop you think they are waiting for,' I whispered.

I looked at the labels. 'This is a philosophy shop,' I said.

'That figures. They look a bit like philosophers. Thinking things. Questions and such. To be or not to be is a pretty good question.'

'Has an inconclusive answer though,' I said.

'Look!' he said, pointing a flappy finger at the throbs. 'This one goes "oompah, oompah, oompah" and this one goes "oompoompoomp", and this one goes "ooompaha, ooompaha, ooompaha". These are the three bears of Frogdom.'

'How long can you keep this up?'

'Oh, a long time,' he said. 'Do you know what they remind me of? Three tuba players working from different sheet music.'

I sighed. My uneasiness was going. I went back to the desk and propped my elbow on it so he could easily look round. He flapped his arms. 'Hey! How about some space.'

I stretched out and pushed the notebooks aside and leaned back in the chair, tilting it – and almost kept right on going over on my back.

For there, standing in the doorway, come from nowhere, was a girl.

'Holy cow!' I said, coming back to the floor with a thump.

'Watch your language,' she said.

'Are you for real?' I said.

'I've got a copyright that says 1986.'

'No,' I said, getting up, advancing, taking her in. 'Listen . . .' She was just full of beans you could see, hardly able to keep it contained. Short hair, skirt to the floor, Indian print, flimsy top with bare shoulders the colour of ovaltine.

Mickey-Mack was going 'Mmm, Mmm.' He had his tongue in the corner of his mouth and his eyes were crossed. He seemed to be hyperventilating.

'Behave,' I said.

He brought his tongue full centre but his eyes were still crossed.

She tapped his nose with her finger like in the old black-and-white movies where the pretty girl has to get rid of her ash.

'Him I've heard about,' she said.

'Careful of the nose,' I said. 'It's just been painted.'

'I had one like him once,' she said. 'He was made from an old sock.'

'An old sock!' Mickey-Mack said in a very small voice. Then louder: 'AN OLD SOCK!'

'Well he wasn't so well put together as you are. But he was a bit like.'

'An old sock,' Mickey-Mack murmured before turning away and tucking his hands into his armpits.

'Now look what you've done,' I said. 'He's not going to speak for hours.'

'But mine wasn't such an intellectual,' she said. 'Though he could speak some Czech.'

'Czech!' said Mickey-Mack as if he hadn't heard such a distasteful thing in all his life. 'An old sock!'

I tried to take her hand and managed to get hold of a little finger and hung on. INHALED. My God! She was simply delicious.

'No, listen,' I said. 'Where did you come from?'

'Is that a birds and bees question or do you mean right this minute?' When she smiled she bit on the tip of her tongue.

'I mean are you just visiting or have you come to stay?'

'Stay? I've been living here for five months.'

'In this house?'

'Certainly.'

'Yesterday even? Last night?'

'Sure.'

'How could you? Where did you sleep?'

'Do you want me to draw you a map or leave you a trail?'

I started to laugh. So did she.

'Am I glad to see you,' I said. 'I was ageing a month a minute.'

'You must have just started then,' she said.

'What a smart-arse. You can't be Indian.'

'Smile, paleface, when you speak like that.'

I heard someone on the stairs above and turned to see Martin.

'Look what I've found,' I said, holding up her hand by the little finger.

'The great discoverer,' she said, sticking out her thumb. 'Next thing you know he'll be discovering the Ganges.'

'Why the secrets?' I said to Martin.

'No secrets,' he said. 'I just haven't got around to telling you everything yet.'

'But this is priority,' I said.

'He's into the reality question,' she said to Martin. 'He was afraid I'd come with a message from the great beyond.'

'And I wasn't going to sign for it,' I said. 'What they call you anyway when you're at home.'

'Lila,' she said. 'And Lila when I'm out.'

'I'm Michael.'

'I know. I just washed your blue jockeys.'

'My God!' I said. 'Are those two phrases connected.'

'Probably.'

I don't know what was so funny about that but it got laughs.

'You look a lot better,' said Martin.

I felt better I tell you.

'You'd better put me away,' said Mickey-Mack. 'I haven't been given anything to say for ten minutes.'

Lila held her hand to Martin. 'Can you pry this clam off me while he still has one hand occupied. I've got to go to the market.'

'Wait,' I said. 'I'll come and carry your change.'

'Is he up to it?' she asked Martin. 'I don't want to mother-hen him all over the village.'

'I think he'll be all right,' said Martin. 'If he falls down stick a flag on him and we'll send someone over with a wheelbarrow to pick him up.'

She looked me up and down. 'Or a ten litre bucket,' she said.

# 4

# THE THOUSAND-
# PETALLED DAISY

BUT MOTHER-HEN ME she did anyway, sitting me down at a teashop with a bottle of warm fizz while she went up and down the one street filling her cloth bags with groceries. You've heard of a one-horse town? Well this was a one-pig town. Rather one dirty old mother and nine squealing little mucks. They cleaned out the gutters of the dirt road like snow-ploughs, up one side, down the other.

One thing you can say for India: nothing goes to waste. As soon as anything falls to the ground it is examined by, in this order, one: little boys with their belly-buttons sticking out. Two: patient old cows. Three: dogs with vibraphone ribs and scabby backsides. Four: nosy goats. Five: aforementioned pigs. Six: crows never satisfied and vultures always amused. Seven: rats. Eight: flies and creepy-crawlies. Anything that's left after they've checked it over is dried up in the sun within twenty-four hours and blown away by the wind, leaving nothing there but the smell. Which nothing can get rid of.

The teashop I sat at was of mud and bamboo with a fire in a mud oven. Smoke seeped through the thatched roof like steam from a northern manure pile in winter.

Brass urn, movie posters, two long bunches of bananas hanging from the smoke-blackened beam, box of pop bottles, that was it. Two benches outside facing each other. A radio blared and crackled near my ear.

I turned the volume down and the bare-bellied teashop man came and slapped the radio on the lid, turned it up. When he'd gone I turned it down v-e-r-y little. Then a little more. Up he came again, checked it, glanced at me out of the corner of his eye. I jiggled a finger in my ear.

'OK, OK,' he said. 'OK,' waggling his head as if it were a ball bearing loose in its socket.

Across the street was a similar structure but a bit bigger with a crooked sign over the door saying ANANDA EMPORIUM AND CRACKER FACTORY. Outside hung plastic buckets and grass brooms and empty bottles and tin oil lamps. On the roof were thrown about thirty worn-out bicycle tyres. As Lila came out of the shop a procession appeared at the end of the street led by a five-piece band. A bass drum, two kettle drums, clarinet and cornet. Couldn't make out the tune. Something very slow. Behind the band was pushed a black-and-gold painted cart like a barrow-boy's. On it was laid out an old yellow lady covered to her nose in flowers. First dead body I've seen. Strange. Like nothing. Behind came a straggly crowd of people, each one preoccupied with the heels of the one in front of him.

Then I made out the tune. It was, if you can believe it, 'Home Sweet Home'.

When it had gone past Lila came across the road and sat down across from me.

'There's no place like it,' I said.

'Christian,' she explained. 'And button up that fat lip.'

I did as she suggested, except to take a sip of warm soda.

She asked for tea in a glass and, waiting for it, she rummaged in her bag and pulled out a tin grasshopper with a rubber suction-cup on the underside. She pressed it down on to the bench between us, looking down at it askance, until, WHANGO! up it went five feet.

She picked it up and handed it to me. 'Here,' she said. 'For Nataraj. Make yourself a friend.'

Her tea came and she sipped it with her elbow way out, her feet wide apart and one hand, wrist bent, on her knee. She looked as if she was taking a breather after breaking a couple of horses.

'Never,' I said.

'Never what?' she said.

'Never Indian.'

'Oh yes I am,' she said. 'After six thousand years of culture: me.'

'Maybe if I saw you in the proper rig,' I said.

'My daddy's a diplomat,' she said. 'Born in Tokyo, high chair in Beirut, kindergarten in Copenhagen, kid's school in Prague, high school in Paris and London.'

'Maybe that's it.'

'Nothing explains nothing,' she said.

'How d'you like England?'

She shrugged. 'It was all right. I didn't like the fences but I liked the fruit trees.'

'Fences! Fruit trees!'

'And the humpback bridges that send you through the sunshine roof.'

'For a moment,' I said, 'I thought you were in the wrong country.'

'I'm never in the wrong country,' she said.

'He's there now? Your daddy.'

'Uh-huh!' she said, shaking her head. 'Washington. After he sweated blood it was going to be Moscow.'

'Why aren't you there? Don't you like the natives?'

'Love 'em. And the country's great. Montana. Wyoming. Howdy ma'am. Roll your own one-handed with the sack dangling from your teeth. Those crazy radio preachers. Big sky. All those cows.'

She took a sip of her tea. 'Where's your mother?'

'Everyone in India wants to know where my mother is.' I said. 'I don't have one is the short answer.'

'Do you have a longer one?'

'I haven't made it up yet. It's someone you miss, I've heard. But I can't remember her.'

'Where d'you live then?'

'When I'm not at school I live with my aunties.'

'Where's that?'

'Out in the boonies. They live in a bee-loud glade.'

Her lips twitched. 'I've heard of it.'

'That must be the other one,' I said. 'My Aunty Aggi has a thing about Irish poets. She says she once met Yeats but she says the same about Oscar Wilde so you don't know whether he was real or just . . . ecto-plasmic.'

'Plasmic,' she murmured. 'Is he any relation to your friend.'

'I shouldn't think so, though he says he knows all the Micks and Macks – except the Scottish branch of course. As he says, you've got to draw the line somewhere.'

'Does he like your aunty?'

'Huh? Mickey-Mack? Sure. He likes everybody. He's just a show-off, that's all. It runs in the family.'

'I've got so many aunties,' she said.

'I've got two. They're into bees.' I did a bit of my watch-out-for-the-bees dance. 'I have a friend, Andy, who says I've been stung so many times, I'm part bee . . . They go around, my aunties, with big hats and blue bags and nets. Lots of nets . . . They're OK.'

'So how come you're here?'

'It's a long story.'

'Can't you cut it to fit?'

'Well, me and my mate were in North Wales rock climbing. And he said, let's go climbing in Kathmandu, and I said OK. And then he met this girl and disappeared.'

'See!' she said. 'That fits. But still it doesn't explain why you came.'

'Andy Fumbles had set his heart on it. And Mickey-Mack thought he'd like to charm a few snakes.'

She blew out her cheeks and shook her head.

'No, listen,' I said. 'Kathmandu! What a great name. There it was, I had a ticket . . . But they wouldn't let us in.'

'I heard about your split head.'

'Yeah . . . He's a great guy.'

'Martin? He's just hopeless,' she said, smiling. 'And when Nanda is here they really make a couple. Like a refugee centre it is. Full of waifs and strays.'

'What category do I fit in?' I said.

'Beats me. You're one of a kind.'

'One?' I whispered. 'Careful, and speak softly.'

She'd had all my attention but now my eyes strayed to a four-wheeled bullock cart that was coming down the road. In the back was a young Tibetan. His head wobbled about to the motion of the wheels: first the back wheels leaned out and the front wheels leaned in, then the right wheels leaned out and the left wheels leaned in, and then the reverse, and then the repeat. When the cart came up opposite the Tibetan spoke to the driver and the cart stopped and he got off, carrying a neat bedroll. He was just a bit bigger than huge. You put a helmet on his head, a number on his back, pad him up some and you wouldn't be able to push him though a door.

'Hi,' he said. 'Mind if I sit?'

'My God,' I said. 'The Voice of America.'

'Careful how you speak about my Alma Mater,' he said. 'You American?'

'Hell no.' I said. 'It's the pop groups who taught me to speak this way.'

'He's as English as Chinese take-away,' Lila said. 'Have a glass of tea.'

'Yeah well,' he said. 'Thanks.' He sat. 'Where's Darshan, do you know?'

'Over on the island,' Lila said, nodding down the street.

'Who's Darshan?' I said. I was unprepared for their laughter.

'Tell him,' she said.

'How?' he said.

She shrugged. 'I guess you're right. Just wait a bit,' she said to me, nice as could be.

'How is it he can have milk tea,' I said when he was served, 'and I can't. He's yellower than I am.'

He almost smiled.

We introduced ourselves. His name was Lobsang something. Born in exile, educated at the University of Colorado. He was teaching Tibetan kids in Dharmsala when he decided on a trip down just for Darshan.

They finally told me about it. Seems Darshan is when everyone can have a look-in at a saint. People come and look and he looks back and everyone goes away feeling good.

'Except this one's a woman, right?' I said.

'Yes,' Lila said.

'And you came all the way down just to see her,' I said to Lobsang.

'Yeah.'

'How come?'

'What else could I do?' he said. 'At the time Kentucky Fried Chicken was off-limits.'

'What a wise guy. You look like a monk.'

'I am a monk.'

'How come you're a monk?'

'Isn't everyone a monk?'

'I'm not a monk.'

'You're not?'

'Pur-lease,' I said and tried again. 'How come you're a monk?'

'What do you mean, how come I'm a monk?'

'What do you mean, what do I mean? How come you're a monk is what I mean.'

'In Tibet, if you're not something else, you are a monk. It just comes with the territory.'

'Is that right?'

'Yeah. Om Mani Padme Hum. Like that.' Lila was spilling her tea.

'You're putting me on?' I said.

'I guess,' he said.

'Oh,' I said. 'Then that's OK. As long as I know.' We were all grinning. Then, 'This woman,' I said to Lila. 'She's coming to the island tomorrow?'

She shook her head. 'Uh-huh!'

'When then?'

'She's already there.'

'When'd she come?'

'About seventy years ago.'

'You mean she lives in the house?'

She nodded.

'She's staying there now? Right this minute?'

'Yes.'

'My God! Where do they stack you all? Underground in the wine bins?'

The tip of her tongue poked out.

'Seventy years!' I said. 'How old is she then?'

'One hundred.'

After a long time to get it right, I said: 'Wow.' And then to Lobsang, 'Is she famous?'

He thought about it, then said, 'No.'

'Who is she then?' I asked Lila.

'What kind of answer you want?'

'Any kind of answer. She's a little old lady with cross-eyes, or: she plays first flute for Madras Symphony, or: she's someone from the planet Venus. Any answer.'

'Well, first of all she's my mum's mum's mum's mum. Is that right? Three greats anyway.'

'She's your great, great, GREAT grandmother?'

'Yes.'

'Holy cow!'

'All the ladies got an early start,' said Lila.

'What you call her? Gee-gee-three?'

'I call her Mataji, Lakshmi calls her Ma, Om Prakash calls her Amma, Nanda calls her Madre.' She turned to Lobsang. 'What do you call her?'

'Mother,' he said.

'It's all the same,' she said.

'And she's locked up in a room except for a couple of times a year when she comes out and zaps everybody.'

'Do you think he has any idea,' she said to Lobsang, 'how close he is to getting a thick ear.'

'No,' I said. 'No disrespect. Really. I'm serious.' And I was serious too. 'It just seems suddenly astonishing to me that a saint is in my house or maybe I am in a saint's house and no one says anything. My God! How many people in the West have ever met a saint. First it's the tooth fairy, then it's Santa Claus, then . . . listen! There's not much left you believe in by the time you're ready for long trousers. You have any idea what my Aunty Mat or my

91

Aunty Aggi would say if I told them I was living in the same house as a saint? My God! Saints! They must be the world's most endangered species.'

'She's not a saint,' Lila said. 'That's just a word convenient for translation. It has nothing to do with religion, nothing to do with morals.'

'Tell me about her,' I said.

She did a bit of ear-pulling, swirling the dregs of the tea around in the bottom of the glass, looking without attention at the ring of naked children who had gathered about us. In the moment's silence one of the older boys said, to giggles, 'What is your native place,' using up all his English in one go.

Lila said: 'She came here to – how to say, look after? serve? be with? – a man who at that time lived on the island. The man was considered holy and she gave up her house and her husband and her children to come and be with him. That's all one can say really. She gave everything up. She came here. She never left. Even when she was younger she never went out much. She doesn't speak – she took a vow of silence when . . . the . . . man . . . was taken from the island.'

It was enough, really, what she said. You know? I was satisfied for the time being. But something in me anyway wanted to push a little further.

'But if she's considered a saint, she must do good works, guide people, convey something,' I said. 'What she do?'

'Do?' Lila looked at Lobsang. 'What does she do?'

Together they turned to me.

'Everything,' he said.

'Nothing,' she said.

Then, also at the same time, they both pointed at each other.

'He's right,' she said.

'She's right,' he said.

'That closed door,' I said.

'Top floor,' she said, 'Next to mine.'

'Holy cow!'

She gave me a smile you could put on toast or sweeten tea with.

'Listen!' I said. 'Serious. Have you got any more surprises?'

'Who knows what's going to surprise you,' she said.

'Can I see her?' I said.

I heard Lobsang slowly draw in the breath through his teeth.

'Tomorrow,' she said. 'Everyone can see her. She gives Darshan.'

'Up close?' I said. 'I want to see her up close.'

She looked down into her empty glass. I was aware of Lobsang beside us, waiting for her answer.

'I want to see her by myself.' I was a bit surprised too.

'It is hardly likely,' she said. 'Maybe. But probably not. I'll ask.'

Lobsang patted me on the arm. 'After all, what do you have to lose,' he said. 'But she hasn't seen more'n ten people alone in maybe thirty years.'

'And probably won't see you either,' Lila said. 'So don't plan on it.'

But I did. She'd see me, I knew it. I could tell by the way my heart was thumping in my throat. You know something? I think Martin is already distributing those berries. And not to the monkeys, either. To me.

I said I didn't need a nap but they put me down with fresh sheets and I was out before I could straighten my knees. And that was all I remember until I awoke in paradise with a wet smacker right between the eyes.

'I'm new at this lark,' she said, 'so don't blame me if you turn into a frog.'

'I don't think it's going to take,' I murmured, closing my eyes again.

'Only one to a prince,' she said. 'Come. You've got yourself a private Darshan in twenty minutes.'

'No kidding,' I said.

'Come. Take a quick shower to wake up.'

'Will it come off, d'you think,' I said, fingering between my eyes, 'in the wet?'

'Wait for me in my room,' she said from the door. 'I'll come and get you there.'

I took a shower as soon as she'd left. And, on impulse, shaved off my Fu Manchu. It just wasn't making it. And I even put on a clean pair of Levis. Before changing Mickey-Mack to his new pocket I flicked at his face with a wash-cloth.

'Do you mind!' he said, spluttering out his tongue.

'You've got to be neat, Mickey-Mack,' I said. 'We're off to see the wizard.'

Mickey-Mack rolled his eyes. 'Sometimes,' he said, 'I

think that the only part of you that deserves any consideration whatsoever are those two fingers of your left hand which are occasionally inserted into an important head socket.'

'Ah,' I said. 'You just say those nice things because you're afraid one day I'll use you to put a shine on my shoes.'

'What shoes?' he said.

When I came out of the bathroom Hari was there with the inevitable lemon juice.

'Guess what,' I said. 'Mother in her infinite wisdom just did something foolish.'

He looked as if he'd just discovered a big hole where a front tooth should be.

'I'm going to have a private Darshan.'

If I'd hit him across the face with a long dollop of something mucky you could, maybe, understand what he looked like.

'When?' he said in a small voice.

'Few minutes.'

He turned, walked straight out of the room, across the garden and leaned his head against the wall in amongst the roses.

I took a couple of sips on the lemon juice before I went out to him.

'You all right Hari?' I said.

He turned to me, his head tilted up, his eyes down. 'It is not fair,' he said.

'What isn't?'

'You have no interest. You do not seek God. Why does

she see you? To you it is curiosity only. Something to pass time. Why won't she see me when I have given up my life to the Lord?'

'Listen,' I said, but with nothing to say that wasn't insulting. For he was right. I'd run a hundred miles if I thought there was the chance to see God. I mean, I don't understand that stuff. But after all it's not often you get to see a saint. Even if it is in translation.

'Listen!' I said. But still nothing coming.

'I must be unworthy,' he said.

'Listen!' I said. But then gave up. It was time to go anyway. So I went back and sucked up the rest of my lemonade and went up the stairs and sat in Lila's room.

It was a surprise, her room. Bright with sunlight and smelling of flowers and absolutely spotless. Even neat. I sat on the narrow, hard bed which was covered with a blue-and-violet striped blanket, pale colours. Straw mat on the floor. Nothing on the walls except whitewash. No paintings or ornaments except a small bronze dancing Shiva on the window sill.

But the books! My God, she read! Paperbacks, all of them. Poets I'd never heard of, texts I couldn't decipher. Books about mountains, books about the sea, books about journeys, books about . . . how do you describe such books . . . about wonders. Microscopic wonders, telescopic wonders, wonders of the seasons and of the places in the universe which never know seasons. Her CD player had earphones on them like a tank commander's. And her CDs were of just about anything that made sound. From far away, or far back, or far out. Sheet music even, she had.

I was getting an inferiority complex just breathing in the atmosphere.

I picked up a seashell that was holding down some letters.

'Hello, hello,' I said into it.

I put it to my ear. 'Line engaged,' I said as she came into the room.

Just behind her came Om Prakash. He was smiling, I guess, his face still unused to the new configuration. He was holding a white rose just out of bud, the stem still wet from the pot. Carefully he snapped off all the thorns, then offered it to me.

'For Amma,' he said.

'OK,' I said.

Lila took my hand, led me along the hallway and suddenly I was all tippy-toes like a mongoose, cringing in my shoulders and breathing shallow. Suddenly scared out of my head. At the door I made a grin. 'Pip-pip,' I said. But she sobered me up with one look.

'OK,' I said.

She opened the door, leaning in with the knob but not moving her feet.

'Aren't you coming in?' I whispered.

She shook her head, prodded me forward.

Then I was inside in a room that was all light, sun everywhere, birdsong through the windows, and the door closing behind me.

Sitting just out of the sun but facing the window, obliquely away from me, was this old lady. She sat very straight, her head a little bent; straight, and very still. I took a couple of steps, paused, took a couple more. Her hands were in her lap but not clasped; curled a little and open as if waiting for someone to drop something into them. And her head was bent as if she was waiting to see what was going to be dropped there.

Very slowly she raised her eyes without moving her head. How can I say it? I don't know if her eyes were brown or blue or whatever or if they looked young or old. All I can say is that her eyes were the most beautiful, the most beautiful, were the most beautiful eyes I have ever seen in my life.

Suddenly my own filled and I couldn't see her and the next thing I knew was that I was on the floor kneeling beside her, looking down into her open hands, weeping my stupid heart out.

She did not move, not her body, not her hands.

Almost immediately I thought: 'What a stupid ning-nong,' and caught hold, snuffling a bit and smearing the wet over my face. I mean it's been years since I did that. Years.

When I thought I was OK I looked up.

And that did it. Off I went again, really letting myself go this time. No noise, no pain. Just release. For she was smiling. I think. You know what it was? I felt that for the first time in my whole dumb term here was someone who could see me for what I was and could still love me. You know what I mean? No matter what. Not liked me a little bit in spite of all the rubbish. LOVED me. Took me into her heart. It was almost too much for me to bear.

Anyway after a while I started to laugh, still as damp as

can be. After all there's a limit to how much water a body can let go at one time. And it was funny. I saw I had dropped tears down off my nose into her palm, so I stiffened two fingers and dabbed them in the wet. Then I just looked up at her with my two fingers still resting in her wet palm. I just looked at her. And she looked at me.

And everything got very still.

Then after some time I guess something was over because I started to sigh, one big sigh after another, with a little tremble in it.

'Listen,' I said.

And then she did smile. I'm sure. I remembered the white rose finally but for a moment I couldn't think where I'd put it. But then I found it in my hand and I offered it to her and she took it and sort of examined it. She looked at it as if it were the first flower she'd ever seen. And then Lila appeared – how she came into the room I'll never know, walked through the walls I wouldn't be surprised – and brought over a vase with a small mouth and the old lady put the rose in it all by itself. I watched where she put it. My rose. Over by the window. And then Lila brought a jampacked bowl of mixed flowers and put it down on the small table at her side.

Carefully, very carefully, her fingers moving as if over file cards, she selected a red rose, tugged it up out of the bunch and offered it to me. Well, hardly offered. I mean who would want to refuse. It was the biggest rose you've ever seen. The biggest, reddest, openest, smelliest rose you could ever, in your wildest dreams, imagine. Curling its petals and hanging on to its drops of water it was absolutely full of rosyness. A blooming crimson cabbage.

With Lila there I began to feel more at home.

'What about Mickey-Mack?' I said.

I hooked him out of my back pocket, unfolded him and shook him out and – what I thought I was doing I don't know – I took up one of her hands and fit it on her.

'This is Mickey-Mack,' I said.

Her eyebrows went up, and her eyes moved from me to him.

'He's my friend,' I said, wondering how I could ever be so dumb.

'How does it feel,' I said to Mickey-Mack, 'to have someone else handling your affairs for a change?'

Mickey-Mack stirred as if waking up.

'There is no change,' he said.

I mean Mickey-Mack said it. In a voice as sweet and as gentle as a cherub's.

Lila dropped down to the floor and hooked an arm over the Mother's knee. Both of us staring at Mickey-Mack, neither of us daring to look up.

'Listen,' I said.

Mickey-Mack jerked his chin up as if in interrogation.

But it was a long time before anything else came. And when it did come it was a surprise to me I tell you.

'Will you be my friend always?' I said.

The answer when it came was barely audible, but it was clear.

'Yes.'

'Never going away?'

'I shall be with you always.'

I started to choke up again. The back of Lila's hand was tight up against the back of mine. Both of us waiting.

'You must know . . .'

The voice was so soft, so quiet, it was almost like imagination, but even the pauses between the words were filled with communication.

'. . . that which is truly everlasting . . .'

Mickey-Mack dropped his head as if considering the complexity of hands.

'. . . is all that . . .'

I could see the perfume from the rose, would you believe me, see it billowing up about us.

'. . . which perpetually renews itself.'

Always will I remember this smell, this sunlight, the colour of the day. It is the smell and the colour of all that is true. It fills up the room; the whole world is filled with this smell, with this colour. There is no room for anything else . . .

Mickey-Mack tilted his head in a way I've never seen him do before. Almost as if he'd found the key to that business with the descending thoughts. Then he came towards me with his arms out and I took him off her hand and put him on my own.

Lila stirred, stood up.

'Is Mickey-Mack going to get a flower?' I said.

The Mother peered at the bowl of flowers, poked a stiff finger around in it, selected a big yellow daisy, offered it. Before Mickey-Mack took it he bowed his head until it touched her hand. She tapped him on the head with a knuckle as if to say: remember.

Then she might have nodded, for Lila sort of helped me up. Me with a big red cabbage in one hand and Mickey-Mack with a big yellow daisy in his. As if I were the one who was a hundred Lila got me somehow up and out of the room, along the hallway and started down the stairs, holding me by the elbow.

At the bottom of the staircase everyone was gathered on the verandah as if in one of those plays where everyone seems to be waiting for someone important to come in through the french windows. Martin sitting with Lobsang on the couch, Hari with a tray of tea, Om Prakash squatting down against the bars of the cage with his knees up around his ears and blowing on a saucerful of tea.

Lila guided me to my chair under the fan, let me sink into it. Then filled a glass from the clay jug and held her hand out for the rose. I gave it up to her and she stuck it in the glass and put it on the table in front of me where it pulsed and shone like some neon sign for a new casino.

'What about Mickey-Mack's?' she said.

I looked at Mickey-Mack and at the yellow daisy. 'I think he wants to keep it for a while,' I said.

Talk about zonked!

Hari, still not looking too happy, absent-mindedly gave me tea, his eyes taking in the yellow daisy.

'Can I tell them?' Lila said.

'Uh?' I said brightly.

She stuck her thumb in the air and jabbed it upwards, her eyes on the ceiling.

'Sure,' I said, not knowing what she was talking about.

'She spoke,' Lila said.

102

No one had said anything since we had appeared on the stairs. Now the silence deepened.

'To this character,' she said.

'I don't believe it,' said Hari. 'I don't believe it. I don't believe it.'

Om Prakash drained his tea from the saucer, put it carefully under his cup, got up, put cup and saucer carefully on the table, moved over, touched Hari on the arm.

'I don't believe it,' Hari said.

Om Prakash spoke to him in Tamil. And then Hari lost it. He started to speak more and more rapidly in Tamil, turning about on the spot, throwing off Om Prakash's arm. Om Prakash, not touching him but moving him by his presence, got him going slowly towards the door. But he couldn't get him through it.

'Put Mickey-Mack away,' Lila said.

'Sure,' I said. I took the yellow daisy and put it in the water glass with the red rose.

I put Mickey-Mack in my pocket and held out my empty hand for Hari to see. In return he held out his hand, palm towards me, fingers wide, with his other hand he sawed at his wrist as if with a knife.

'I know where it grows,' he said.

Somebody then walked over my grave.


'So what is Yoga then?' I said as I walked between Lobsang and Lila down to the beach. The grove of coconut palms had been planted in rows and the effect was hallucinatory as you passed from one line into another, new diagonal lines always opening up towards the sea.

Lobsang said: 'It's just one damn thing after another.'

'To the West,' said Lila, 'it's the religion where god-liness comes next to cleanliness.'

'It's a religion then,' I said.

'No way,' said Lobsang.

'Just a way of being,' said Lila.

'I thought it was all dark stuff,' I said. 'Aust-erities. Renunc-iation. Sac-rifice.'

'Well, there's that too,' said Lobsang.

'Uh-huh,' said Lila, shaking her head. 'It's all sunlight.'

'Maybe it's changing,' said Lobsang. 'Before it was "All is illusion; let it go." Now it's "All is in order; let it come."'

Which wasn't bad when you come to think of it, though it didn't make much sense. I began to feel as if I had spent a lifetime learning a language so that I could study, say, some book of wisdom and finally they decide I'm ready and I get to open the book and the first words I read are: words will get you nowhere. Yet what else could you use? For all that silence in which everything is under-stood, in which everything is as it should be, was gone. When nothing needed explanation, that was gone. Now everything again clamoured for explanation. Barely an hour after Whack! Whack! Satori, here I was again, con-fused.

'You know,' I said. 'I don't remember the room. I don't know what she wore, nor what she looked like. I can't remember her face. I can't remember her face.'

Lila laughed.

'I can't remember even her face,' I said. 'How can that be?'

'You were too busy looking at something else,' she said.

'I can't even remember her face,' I said. 'Only the eyes.'

What does she do, I had asked. And one had said: nothing, and the other had said: everything.

But what could she do, an old woman, silent, in a room by herself, even though conscious, knowing, what could she do, only now and then coming out. What could she do? Change the world, for God's sake?

'I still don't know what she looks like,' I murmured.

'Martin's got some photographs,' Lila said, still laughing.

'I'll ask him,' I said, but absently.

For I was beginning to understand Hari's anguish. I loved her though what the hell was I loving when I could not even remember her face! But she had been sprung on me new, not prepared for, not leading, as far as I knew, anywhere, and though I didn't know what to do with it I could at least enjoy it. For Hari it was different, a different thing, not depending on the beauty of the eyes, a thing based on belief, secure, leading to the inevitable. When doubt comes to me I can handle it, for I know doubt's business is to doubt, whereas Hari's doubt can shake his universe. Good intentions do not transform, I wanted to say to Hari (and don't ask me where that comes from), only love does.

Love! My God! What do I know about love. I only know about turn-ons. And getting-off . . .

'So then how do you start this yoga bit?' I said.

'You start to search for what has already been found,' said Lobsang.

I stopped in my tracks so that they had to stop too.

Both looking at me. Hell! Here was this flat-faced, yellow, bald-headed kid who mumbled his words like through a hot fudge sundae and he comes out with something like that.

'Talk about fortune cookies,' I said.

'I'm a conservationist,' he said, as if in apology. 'I recycle everything I've ever been told.'

I was, I admit, afraid to ask for more.

I started up again and we walked out of the coco-palms, down the slope of the white beach, until we came close to the water. The way I was feeling, had Lila not stopped, we'd have kept on going, walking, I betcha, all the way to Sri Lanka on top of the waves.

Lila kicked off her flip-flops and looked up at the sky. The clouds were lower and higher, both, reaching up to a stupendous white height, turning over within themselves, pressing down it seemed upon the earth with all their stupendous weight.

'Listen!' she said, stealing my line.

The sea roared with messages from way out beyond the horizon, mumbled and thumped and promised more and acted tough. Way out it seemed confused with no white water but moving into long and sullen swells as it approached land. A hundred metres offshore must have been a sand-bar for here the waves curled high and transparent before thundering down and levelling out, foam-patterned in green and white.

In two fluid movements Lila unbuttoned and dropped her clothes and in her white bikini took the few steps to the sea. My heart turned over like the sea, like the clouds.

I wanted to race in there and show off, splash water, dive around, fool about, feel that touch of slippery cold skin in that rushing sea.

Lobsang, pulling his swimming trunks up under his robes, had a more difficult time of it, folding everything, turning in all the tabs, laying everything out just so. Then he too was in, passing Lila in a great Yankee splosh, arms flat and wide and strong as hell. He was OK. But I was better. I was good. I have to admit it don't I if it's the truth? If it's the only thing I'm good at?

Lila was OK too, no dainty business with the chin up but head down and a wide open twisted mouth and her great legs thrashing.

I'd promised Martin to stay dry so I turned and walked along the beach ankle-deep, kicking the water ahead of me. It fell in sparkling drops. Even this close-in it pulled some, the water, the current sliding north along the beach. But not too strong to handle.

Listen! There it was again, that silence behind the roar of the sea. That silence in which everything rests, to which everything returns. Next to love, quietness; next to bliss, peace. Martin had said it, admitting a bit sadly to the coming-on of the years and the lowering of the aims.

The beach was white sand, coarse with small pebbles which rolled back down the scalloped edge of land. Small highwater crabs cleaned out their holes; others, covered up, bubbled as the water receded. Head down, kicking my feet, the water and the wet sand lightening and darkening before my gaze as the sun came and went through the clouds.

When I turned back I saw that Lila and Lobsang were standing together knee-deep in the water looking out into the waves. Something turned over within the water as it lifted and prepared to break. It broke, rushed up, hushed back, taking whatever it held back into itself. It was grey-ish, the thing borne in, long as a man, turning over, not on the surface, not on the floor, hanging midway between floor and surface.

By the time I got back to them it was in the shallows. The body of a man it was, sure enough. What was left of a man. Water-whitened, shapeless, eyes gone, fringes of flesh, flopping over, pulling back, loose and rubbery, heavy with water. Lila and Lobsang withdrew from the sea.

We stood indecisively for some moments before Lobsang went up the beach and brought back two sticks of driftwood. He re-entered the water and stood near the thing with the sticks in his hand, no one helping him. As it came up with the waves he stuck the sticks in the sand behind it, holding it, keeping it from being sucked back in by the rush of water. When the waves came back and moved it higher, he moved the sticks again.

While he was doing this Hari appeared, coming through the trees. Slowly he walked down the beach and stood with us for a moment. Then he stepped into the sea, a bit bossy, pulled out a stick and prodded the thing back into deeper water.

Lobsang, contesting the other stick, started to protest but Lila touched his arm.

'Whatever was there,' she said, 'has gone.'

He considered, one hand on the stick, then let it go and stepped back.

'It's not clean,' said Hari. Lobsang was seriously cool and seemed undisturbed, though he looked as if he had plenty to say. But he kept quiet.

'Tomorrow is Darshan day,' Hari said.

Never one in seventeen years that I can remember and then two in one day, would you believe it. The first one was OK, a little old lady in a box with lots of flowers, her chin held up by a handkerchief with a tidy knot at the top of her head, and the trumpet going Home Sweet Home. But this was different. This was something else.

Shapeless, fingers, toes, ears and nose, his pecker pretty much gone, nibbled away, with suckerfish at the sockets. Grey, could be anyone. Wound at the throat, enormous belly, a grin sort-of, as if he was amused by the whole affair. And not a stitch on him except that red string they tie, that rag that makes their underpants.

What happened, I wondered. Fell off a boat? Clobbered and just left? Walked in? All these questions. Trying to be flip. But failing. Two in one day. And one that will last me forever.

Just imagine him. Swishing about, wiggly things exploring him, getting smaller all the time, losing his shape, getting insignificant, eventually dissolving like something cooking. I mean he looks creepy. Men are temporary creatures aren't they? Transitory?

Patiently while we three stood without speaking with the water only now and then covering our feet, Hari, now with a stick in each hand, guided the thing down the length of the beach. Where the river entered the sea we could tell that the current would take it away from the land again. Hari was already standing still, watching it drift.

'Everything seems to have picked up speed,' I said, not knowing what I was talking about. But both Lila and Lobsang nodded.

Lila sat down on the sand at the edge of the water and hugged her knees. Lobsang sat next to her. I joined them, tilting on one cheek to keep Mickey-Mack out of the wet. But that wouldn't work so I took him out.

'Hey, I've got goose bumps,' I said. But no one answered. Talk about calling out into the void!

The body, way out now, dipped and rolled in the waves, sometimes disappearing altogether. We waited in silence till long after the body was gone. Hari had come back and sat behind us. How can it be that someone, out of sight, not saying anything, can be so loud. I mean loud.

The sea rolled and thumbed, its spray wetting our faces.

I got up and stuck another stick in the sand just out of reach of the waves, and arranged Mickey-Mack on it.

'You mind, hear?' I said.

His arms drooped crossways but he didn't say anything.

I stepped into the clean-looking sea, then deeper in. When I was up to my thighs I started to scrub my hands together, then my arms and my legs, then cupping my hands and bringing up water into my face and over my shoulders. Over and over until my shorts were soaking.

Suddenly I was in, exuberantly streaking out from shore, full out, arms flashing, legs like nothing, green water against my eyes. Thirty metres flat out then legs up and shooting down down down. Touching bottom, two fistfuls of sand, legs bent, thrust, and up up up, some tremendous buoyancy, shooting up towards the light. Then exploding into sunlight, wide-open in joy, out of the water, waist high, fistfuls of sand pattering on the surface of the sea.

And Lila and Lobsang racing out towards me.

'You scared us stiff,' Lila said when they got close. 'You're supposed to be sick.'

'You swim good,' said Lobsang.

'Isn't that the truth?' I said.

'Come on in now,' Lila said, swimming around me like a cocker spaniel to get between me and the open sea.

'OK,' I said.

I got on her left when we turned for shore, breathing on the wrong side, so we could see each other as we came up for air. And we took our time and did it slow, timing our arms, coming up at the same time, and so we came in together until, bellies to the sand, we ran out of sea.

Lobsang came up the other side and we lay there, elbow to elbow, with the water surging around us and streaming from our bodies, all of us panting a bit, me much more than them.

When Hari came up in his wet dhoti he seemed puzzled by the way we were looking.

'Come on in,' I said. 'Get clean.'

He shook his head.

'It's a big ocean,' I said. As if that explained anything.

'All things decay in it,' he said.

'It's not like that,' I said. 'It purifies everything.'

'No,' he said.

'Can you swim?' I said.

'No.'

'Want me to teach you?' I said.

'No,' he said.

He tucked up his dhoti and squatted just at the limits of the sea. Taking up a seashell he reached well in front of him to draw in the wet sand. His thoughts seemed to be far away. He drew a daisy, then scribbled the seashell through it. A wave came and erased it. He did it again, and again a wave came and erased it.

'M-Mum-Michael,' he said. 'I believe you.'

'That's OK,' I said, not understanding a thing.

'Om Prakash is going to ask the Mother for a private Darshan for me this day itself.'

'That's good,' I said.

He draw again a daisy in the sand, scribbled it over as before, waiting for the wave.

'I am going to stay here for ever,' he said. 'And never leave her.'

He seemed to be waiting, his shell ready, but this time the sea did not come.

'Miss Lila,' he said. 'Om Prakashji said I should tell you . . . that I am sorry.'

She threw a pebble at him. 'OK,' she said.

He stood up, shook out his dhoti, brushed his hands free of sand. 'I can take your leave?'

'See you later,' I said.

We watched him go up the beach and into the trees.

'I don't know how long I can stand this,' I said, 'with all this sand shwooshing up my shorts.'

'Where'd you learn to swim like that?' Lobsang said.

'Never in England,' Lila said.

'I did too,' I said. 'In an indoor pool that gave me pink-eye and green hair and blue . . . lips.'

'My father said I'd never learn to swim,' Lobsang said. 'He said a man should stay in his own element. For me that meant mountains.'

'You're not so bad,' I said.

'I never thought I'd get the breathing right. It was worse than pranayams.'

'You're not so bad either,' I said to Lila.

'That's because I wasn't trying,' she said.

Mickey-Mack seemed despondent, slumped down on his stick, his arms crossed and his head twisted. 'I hope he's all right,' I said, nodding towards him.

'He's all right,' Lila said.

'How do you know,' I said. 'He hasn't said anything for over an hour.'

'He gave me a smile.'

'He did?'

She nodded, her chin on the backs of her hands.

'When?'

'Just now.'

I gave her a long look. I mean a L-O-N-G look. She nudged me with her shoulder.

'Oh, that's all right then.' I nudged her back.

'Excuse me,' said Lobsang, 'for intruding and everything.' He gave us his back and reclined on one elbow, supporting his head with a hand.

Lila gave her first real laugh of the day and told him not to be that way. Then she got up as I went to take Mickey-Mack off his stick and she gave a hand to Lobsang to pull him up.

Then we went back to the house.

# 5

# LONG WALKS AMONG
# THE CLOUDS

WHEN WE GOT BACK I was on my own. A lot of ooltah-pooltah and me. 'Get lost,' Lila said after I had taken my shower and came out again ready for anything. She just pushed me into a corner with a tray of toast and boiled chicken and carrots, a thermos of soup, and a bowl of curd and honey. I all but licked the plate.

There'd been a regular clean-up going on all afternoon with extra people from the village, not only in the house but all around, trees being trimmed of low branches, leaves being raked. There were men still strengthening the footbridge and old, old ladies dusting the stones, it looked like, around the shrine. Busy as bumbles as long as there was light.

Later ('Look what you've started,' Lila said), there was almost a procession of people going upstairs.

First Om Prakash went. And when he came down he was a sight, I tell you. He looked like an Indian woman who had just found out she was to give birth to Kalki. I mean he was so radiant he had changed colour. He came up to me and held both my hands together in his, his eyes all wet, and just smothered me to bits.

Then his wife and son went up, and when they came down the child was all shy with his arms about her neck and his face buried in her shoulder. She looked just about as she always did only more so: happy and comfortable and pneumatic.

Then Martin went up. And he was up there a long time. And when he came down he was serious, I tell you. He was so serious that he seemed afraid to move. But no wet eyes on him. For some time he stood at the bars of the cage looking up at where the monkeys had retreated, then he leaned forward and pressed his forehead against the bars.

When he finally straightened up and turned I said, 'I'd like to see your photographs.'

He looked at me as if I had suddenly materialised out of a cloud of radioactive smoke.

'Dr Faustus, I presume,' I said. But it skittered right past.

'I will bring,' he said, just like a babu.

And he did, going right up and bringing them down. They were in an album bound in pale blue cloth and covered in plastic. When he gave it to me he didn't say anything but he somehow conveyed the idea that if I left a thumbprint on it he'd have my tripes. And when he turned away I felt sure that he'd be gone till morning.

As I opened the book I saw Lila lead Hari upstairs. The way he was walking he'd lost six inches of height and the look on his face was as if he couldn't believe he was finally going to make it. But he didn't lag behind any.

The photographs were a surprise. For the woman I had seen was not represented there.

There were thirty or so photographs in the book, one to a page, dated, one to a year. In all the prints she was sitting in the same chair, the chair was in the same place, the light coming through the window suggested the same time of day. Her pose was more or less as I had seen her. Her feet, I saw now, were on a pillow, one elbow usually on the arm of the chair, her hands usually in her lap, palms up.

But each photograph seemed unlike any other. And none like the picture in my mind.

She was, it seemed, a small woman, pale, slender but not, even in her latest photos, with that excessive thinness which sometimes comes with old age. She never looked her age. In the early photos her hair was black in braids, in the later ones grey then white but still thick, in a bun; always it was pulled back from her face which was unwrinkled. Her eyes . . . her eyes were lovely, sure, yet not as I remember them. Dark they were and wide, and wide apart, and I could see how one could get lost in them . . . and yet . . . Sometimes she wore a sari, sometimes one of those pyjama outfits. Sometimes she looked grave and sometimes she looked joyful. But that isn't what I mean when I say she always looked different. And it had nothing to do with the passage of time. The face was the same but the message was different. No. The force was the same but the woman was different. Not that either. I turned the page with the last photograph, smoothed down the blank page on which this year's photograph would go. There weren't many pages left, I noticed. Time passed as I looked down on to the empty page. I don't know how long it would have been before I moved if Hari had not come down and distracted me.

I've never seen such a dopey look on anyone's face in all my life – well at least not since the time, not so long ago, when I came down myself. He just didn't know what to do with himself. He'd go outside, walk about, come in and light up a whole packet of incense, sticking them all over in the unlikeliest places so that someone or other was always burning himself. Then you'd hear him out in the back garden chanting mantras. Then he'd go out again to take another bath in the river. Re-dedication was writ large across his brow.

Everyone that evening wanted to be alone. I had a long conversation with Mickey-Mack who was the only one willing to talk to me. He had some interesting things to say, like: 'The English have form but no content unlike the Indians who have content but no form.' But then he dug under the skin a bit. 'You are a member of a thrifty race,' he said. 'Half the time out to save your skin, half the time out to save your face.' Which, as I didn't ask for it, got him folded up pretty quick.

I saw Lila briefly at the top of the stairs and whistled up at her. But she said, 'No chance,' so I went outside. If I wasn't careful Hari and I would be like a pair of wired-up rats always bumping into each other as we worked our way through our neurotic maze. Relax, I said, relax.

Someone must have heard me, for when I went and sat upon a rock on the river bank, legs crossed even, I was as loose as a fireside cat on a winter's night. You couldn't see the river for you couldn't see the stars, the limits of vision brought in close by the heavy clouds. The night was very still and pressing down upon the land squeezing out of it a dry smell as if of burning, or of harvest . . .

Children on the high banks of the river were lighting sparklers and winding them furiously in circles so that they looked like wheels of fire. The sound of their laughter seemed to travel miles over water before it reached me . . .

The top floor of the house was all lit up, Lila's room and the other one, every window open, the light shining down on the top of the yellow-flowered tree . . .

I wonder whether I'll ever grow up before I grow old, I thought. (Lord, let me grow up, but not yet.) I must admit I don't want to give up anything, even youth, though I guess the passage of time will take care of that. Sacrifice! I suppose that's what's troubling Hari. He wants to offer up something but he doesn't feel he's got anything that the Lord would want. What a concept! I give up something (usually something I can do without) in the hope of getting something else (usually something I want a lot). A bargain. The only good kind of sacrifice, surely, is when you are increased by it, not diminished by it. As in love. There sacrifice is nothing special, merely something that love expects.

Guess who's just come up, standing near me but not seeing me, his feet almost in the water? He drops back his head, turns out his palms at his thighs, and starts to chant softly. Sanskrit I suppose. It is very beautiful but his voice comes from high up and is kind of constricted. It is perhaps lacking in that joy which the words, I bet my boots, require. The voice becomes a plea, insistent, desperate almost, and . . . how to say it ... deadly.

I awoke to find that during the night I had been changed into a man. (Kafka got it all wrong.)

Since my illness I had been waking late but this morning I awoke to the crowing of the village cocks. Mentally I was not at my best though physically I felt great: it was the first night I hadn't had those sweats and those willie-willie dreams. I lay there for a while exploring my new dimensions and as soon as the sun came up I got out of bed and went and looked in the mirror. There it was all right, what I didn't particularly want to see right now, not yet, a certain look in the eye, a thickening around the jaw, stubble on the upper lip.

An early morning dove mourned for me outside my window.

Not that I had lost my sense of the ridiculous. After all someone who spends much of his waking hours in conversation with a black and woolly glove with rolly eyeballs can't just be straightened out in any hour before breakfast.

But still it was a bit of a shock. I mean I thought I'd got a long time to go yet. I got under the cold shower while I contemplated the future.

My God! I could just see it.

Looking over your shoulder, smelling under your arm, drying between your toes.

My God!

Cutting some cracker out, setting some bird up, putting some kid down, pulling more bread in.

My God!

Worrying about waistcoats and booties without laces and Irish fishermen's hats that look like saggy woolly mushrooms, and about the stripes on your tie and the cuffs on your shirt and the taper on your trouser leg. Even about the fit of your underpants.

My God!

Remembering to open doors, and when the red and when the white, and what's in and what's out, and how to find the quickest way up and the longest way down.

My God!

Have I got to learn all those stupid rules and play those stupid games and fret about image and prowess and act tough or smooth depending on what's coming up, trying always to be the fancy dancer one trick ahead of exposure . . .

Om Prakash must have heard the shower for there he was looking in the window.

'Om Prakash,' I shouted over the splash of water. 'Something terrible's happened. I've grown up.'

'Are you sure?' he said, looking worried.

'A big black bird came in the dark and settled on my chest and all night long he pecked at my vitals and said "CONFORM".'

'To be in agreement,' Om Prakash said, 'is to differ with the Lord.'

I almost wept. There it was. That was why I loved it

here. Never what you expect; always what you need.

'What would you like for breakfast?' he said.

I turned the water off while I soaped myself. 'Three fried eggs and about twelve greasy strips of bacon. Lots of butter on my toast. And a big pot of strong coffee.'

'Right,' he said. 'Haribhai is being difficult today, that's why I have come. He has given notice to Mr Martin. He says from now on he will serve only the Mother.'

'How is it you seem so calm and understanding today whereas yesterday you were all up for putting him down.'

'Today the needs are different.'

'Yours or his?'

'That is a good question . . . But he's a bit of a trouble at the moment. First he gives up all the work except that which she specif-ically demands of him. Then he wants to sleep on the floor outside her door. Then he wants to see her every day so that she can instruct him in his daily routine. Oyo! I think it is going to be a lot of work for her now he's promised to dedicate his life to her service.'

'The next thing you know he'll be nailing some proclamation to your front door.'

'Yes, but what will he say on it?'

'I don't know but it will be at least ten pages.'

'I was once told of a man who searched for the perfect tree so that he could build in it a place above the turmoil of the world where he could worship God. And when he had found it, he came with his servant and built himself a platform high in the branches. Every day the servant went and brought what was needed and put it in a basket and the basket was hauled up. The arrangement did not last long however.'

'He fell out of bed or what?'

'It was the servant. He got tired of walking through all the filth that was cast down from the tree . . . So the man had to come down and start somewhere else. His days were filled with the search for the perfect tree, a willing servant, and God. In that order.'

I turned the water back on to rinse myself.

'I'll get your fried eggs,' Om Prakash said, leaving.

Although I didn't need it I'd thought I'd better shave again as a concession to the requirements of my new maturity.

When Om Prakash came back he didn't want to stay as he didn't have the time. He would be busy, he said, for the rest of the morning.

'Just one thing,' I said. 'About Lila . . .' But I didn't know what I wanted to ask.

He waited patiently.

'Five months she's been here, right?'

'Perhaps five months.'

'And working . . .'

When he saw that I didn't know where to go, he said: 'She had been out of India for a couple of years. Suddenly she decided she wanted to spend time with Amma. She came. Stayed on. She keeps putting it off, her return.'

'How old is she?'

'One hundred years.'

'No. Lila.'

'Oh Lila!' He made a gesture with his open hand as if throwing something over his shoulder. 'She's that age where age is unimportant. I'm reminded of something my gentleman said to me: "How old would you be, if you didn't know how old you were." I like that.'

He told me that Darshan was at ten o'clock, and that if I went outside I would see where it was by all the people waiting. And then he left.

When I had finished my breakfast (tea with lemon, toast with yellow jam, curd with honey), I too went outside.

The sky was overcast, without shape. Silken seeds floated in the air. Clouds of parrots were in extreme agitation, forming and re-forming flights and shrieking as they clung in clusters on the trees like loud exotic fruit. The sea boomed on the beach.

A few people all dressed in white were coming across the repaired footbridge and some were picking their way across the dry river bed. A small overloaded boat was setting off from the other bank of the river. It was only nine o'clock and yet already it seemed that a hundred had come. The small shrine was buried in a mound of flowers and was hazy from the smoke of burning incense.

I walked on round the house and then stopped in absolute amazement. For in a wide area, packed tight across almost the whole island, was a whole throng of people. Not hundreds but thousands. Thousands. All silent and sitting with hardly a movement, all facing the house. New arrivals came, found space, put down their mats or newspapers or squares of plastic, sometimes lit up a stick of incense to stick in the earth before them, then settled themselves and became still like those all about them.

Above the cage the three top windows on the side of the house facing us were open, each leading on to a kind of Romeo-and-Juliet balcony; the centre one had a yellow cloth thrown over the railing.

I walked through the crowd, here and there, on among the trees where there were fewer people. I saw Lobsang sitting alone in meditation. I sat down next to him but it was fifteen minutes or more before he opened his eyes. I had plenty of time to give shape to my thought.

I gave him space to blink and work his mouth and recognise me, then I gave it to him. Klop!

'Don't you wish that what was beyond thought was also beyond words,' I said.

He blinked again. 'The more ungraspable the concept,' I went on, enjoying my advantage, 'the more imaginative the argument.'

'Well,' he mumbled, as if he was considering some complexity in the baseball scores, 'all things begin in wonder.'

The advantage he has over me, of course, is that he does not think before he speaks.

'Are there always this many?' I said.

'I hear there are more and more every year,' he said, his tongue still sounding as if it were unaccustomed to form words.

'My God!' I said. 'What would happen if they advertised?'

'The reputation of a holy man seldom gets less,' he said. 'Except after his death. And not often then. And that goes for holy women too.'

'I've never heard of a holy woman before,' I said.

'You can have a holy anything. Holy people, holy stones, holy cows, holy pools, holy snakes, holy termite mounds, holy trees. Even, so I've heard, holy English milestones.'

'Holy Englishmen?' I said.

'I don't think I could go that far,' he said.

Faintly there was a low sound that might have been thunder. People nearby looked at each other and then up at the sky, which had began to darken.

Then I saw Lila making her way through the crowds and although she had seen us I stood up and waited and watched her. She was wearing one of those pyjama things, white with embroidered flowers down the bib. She carried a small bunch of yellow flowers, marigolds. Her hair was all soft and flopped about as she walked.

I held her hand as she came up but when she sat down between Lobsang and me she took it away. She gave Lobsang a flower and he took it and with it between his palms he touched his thumbs to his chest. Then she gave one to me. Then she put one in her lap and leaned forward and tapped the woman in front of her on the arm and gave her the rest. The woman tilted her head in thanks while accepting them, keeping one and passing the others on.

Then, with no nonsense, Lila settled herself down with her legs crossed and her back straight and her neck stretched. I don't know why it shook me when she closed her eyes. I suppose it was that I felt she had become inaccessible. That she had gone to a place I couldn't go to with her. And that she could be happy there.

I could see the pulse ticking in her throat; her eyes moved beneath her lids; the moisture dried on her lips. When she breathed I couldn't see the rise and fall of her breast.

She wasn't gone long but even so when she came back she was still a little remote. Lovely and smiling and cheerful, but a little remote.

I took a sniff at the flower and tucked it behind my ear.

I don't know how it started, but here and there people began to get to their feet, until all were standing.

It was getting closer to the hour of Darshan and time seemed to thicken, not slow down but somehow it seemed to strengthen, become significant. The small balcony with the yellow cloth became the focal point for ten thousand people, concentration beaming in on the window at which she would appear.

Just before ten o'clock a tremendous clap of thunder surprised everyone into laughter.

Then she was there.

You could see Om Prakash's hands at her waist from behind as she made the one step to the balcony. Then she was free. Two bird-steps to the rail, a slight frown as she put her hands out and settled herself there. Then a slow look around: down over the edge, up and around, taking everyone in. No smile, no gesture. Almost as if she were alone, examining the ground for the tracks of some huge, nocturnal dragon. Then, everyone looked at, she raised her head and looked out beyond the trees, out to where the sea rhythmically beat.

I think we all ceased to breathe.

Without blinking, without moving, she simply stood there and looked, gazing, it seemed, into a place not yet discovered, seeing cities not yet built, lands not yet explored. Universes, even, not imagined.

Then . . . tip . . . tip . . . tip tip . . . tip tip . . . tip tip tip . . . began the rain. Gently, without wind, after a long time, the rain, easement to the dry earth.

Slowly, after seeming to be unaware of the raindrops, she brought her gaze back from that distant place, tilted up her head. And then she did something that made me laugh. With the rain dropping on to her face she held her hand out as if to confirm it. But my laughter ceased as she remained like that with her head back and one hand out. And the rain coming down.

Then she dropped her hand and, rather stiffly, looked back sort of under her chin at Om Prakash standing just inside the room. He came up as if to help her back but, almost impatiently, she gestured him forward until he was at her side. She raised her hand, fingers up and stiff, cracked at the wrist, and placed it on Om Prakash's upper arm. Once more she looked down and around at the crowd, into, it seemed, every eye. And then, quite deliberately she tapped his arm a couple of times.

The woman in front of us gave a kind of whimper. But that was the only sound I heard. Except for the sea.

Om Prakash looked as if he'd run out of script. He simply stood looking down at her until she finally reached for his hand and turned. Very slowly, very slowly, now like an aged, aged woman, she moved back into the room and out of our sight.

For a moment no one stirred. Then a ripple went through the crowd as hands were raised to the chest and forehead, and everyone was almost immediately back to normal. The bustle of picking up their gear, laughing at the rain, some already running to beat the crowd.

Is that it? Is that all there is? What did it mean? What did they see? What, in fact, had happened just now? And if it was something that was done, why does she do it? . . . Why does she do it? And for whom does she do it? . . . But it was only part of me that was asking: part of me knew.

Thunder again. Rolling and deep, prolonged, reverberating. The clouds now really dark, pressing together, picking up movement, acquiring substance.

Lobsang took up his bedroll and shifted it to his shoulder and together we walked back on the edge of the crowd towards the house. At the beginning of the footbridge the crowd was backed up, in good humour but pushing a bit, covering up their heads, examining the stains of the water on their clothes. Hari was there like a riverboat tout. Any minute you expected him to shout 'all aboard' or some Tamil equivalent.

It would take hours for everyone to cross and many, all the young, were running and leaping across the river bed. Already the water was filling the hollows, was beginning to find its way under the footbridge. Down at the beach a moving curtain of grey was obliterating the landscape.

Lobsang gave a hitch to his bundle, considered the

crowd and the way across the river bed and had already seemed to have made up his mind when he saw Om Prakash standing in the gateway to the house.

Immediately he went over to him and stood quite still in front of him. Said something. Both looked at each other very seriously. Then Lobsang held his hands to his chest and made a deep and formal bow. Om Prakash twitched his hands at his thighs before replying with a similar gesture. I'd never seen Lobsang look so strong or so serious. I've never seen Om Prakash look so sad.

His hands twitched again at his thighs and then he turned and went through the gate.

The thunder was now almost continuous, and the rain heavy as Lila and I, taking Lobsang with us, followed Om Prakash into the courtyard.

# 6

# THE WAY OF SMOKE,
# THE WAY OF WATER

JUST INSIDE THE GATE Martin was standing on a stool, cutting the fibres which held in place a large bamboo panel. His heart didn't seem to be in it and his indecisiveness made Lobsang and me pause to see if he needed any help. But he didn't. He was doing what he wanted to do.

He got down off the stool and we joined him there, the three of us standing in a row just out of the wet, dopey-looking it must have seemed, like a frozen frame of the Three Stooges just before they turn and start hitting each other on the head. All in a dumb row looking up at the rain, Martin particularly rapt, as if counting drops.

I stood it as long as I could, then gave in: 'Lob, all this wordlessness is giving me goose bumps. I can see it leading only to mindlessness.'

Martin gave himself a kind of shake. 'That is quite profound,' he said.

'It is?'

'It is.'

'How can it be profound with me knowing nothing about it?'

'Profundity is always suspect when you can understand it fully,' he said.

'Give me a break, will you,' I said. 'I never have this kind of trouble with my other buddies.' I turned from him and shouted up at the monkeys. 'All right you guys. Get your things together. Almost time to go.'

Already slicked down with the rain, they blinked and hugged themselves, their hands stuck in their armpits and legpits.

'Another hour and we'll be safe for another year,' Martin said.

'Wouldn't you know it. Out of a job before I carve my first footnote.'

'Well, it will look good on your CV,' he said.

'Come on!' I said, covering my rear. 'You don't really think I went along with all that monkey business, do you?'

'Why would you ever not?'

'What was there to believe?'

'That makes three questions in a row,' he said. 'Asking a question in answer to a question is always a good way to question the answer.'

I laughed. 'I'll have to try that out on Mickey-Mack. He's a great one for unanswerable questions and question-able answers.'

'He'd be wordless,' Lobsang said.

'Not him. Mindless maybe but not wordless. But come to think of it he hasn't spoken to me for hours. I think he's beginning to look upon me as brain-damaged.'

I took him out and blew into him so that his arms shot out like La Bohème. He didn't like that one bit, grumbling that it rearranged all his innards so that he didn't know what went where. But when we got him all unwrinkled he had a good look around.

'So? As the ducks said to Noah.'

'Forty more days to go.'

'I can't wait. Who are those wet gents?'

'They're just leaving to catch a cold.'

'Why don't they wait in the garage?'

'You're just full of questions.'

'Isn't there a song about that? Some foreign fella who makes a stab at English? "The question, my friend, is dangling in the wind." Something like that.'

'I fancy you've been eavesdropping,' I said.

'I couldn't help it. They don't make trousers like they used to.'

'So I don't have to warn you about the question that answers questions.'

'As long as the answer is right who cares if the question is wrong.'

'You've been saving that one up, haven't you?'

'Yoohoo,' he sang out, at the monkeys, waving his stubby arms. 'Hopeless! They don't even have enough sense to came in out of the stuff.'

'They've got short memories. They can't remember what it does or how long it goes on.'

'Like life,' he said.

'You getting into parables?'

'Yes,' he said. 'Madame Blavatsky and her monkey. Androcles and the lion. A bit of this, a bit of that. The way to go.'

'I just love you when you're coherent.'

Martin waved a hand as if he was conducting something intricate. 'How does one break into this, once you've got going?'

'Easy really,' I said, 'you just put Mickey-Mack on the defensive.'

'I think,' said Lobsang, 'I met his brother, Big Mac, in Colorado. Underneath the arches.'

'That's the idea,' I said. 'But now he's offended. I'll have to fold his ears. That's the only way to stop his eyes rolling up like that . . . No more eavesdropping mind.'

Immediately Martin tried to get back. 'What did you have trouble with?'

'Where were we? Let me put that differently: where are we?'

'Trouble believing about the monkeys.'

'I didn't have any trouble. Actually I can live better with things I don't believe in than I can with things I believe in. Then I know exactly where I am – unsure of everything.'

'Much of it was true.'

'Like a little bit pregnant?'

He looked surprised. 'You're right. If it is not all true then it is false.'

'False, schmaltz – as long as it's all right on the Sabbath.'

Neither of us, clearly, was willing to come right out with anything.

'I thought you needed to stay a while longer,' he finally said, obliquely.

'Longer than what?'

'I thought it would take longer then it did.'

'What take longer?'

But it was hopeless. 'I'm glad you saw her,' was all he said.

Absently he brushed the rainwater from his hair, fidgeted a bit, made noncommittal movements with his hands. But saying nothing more.

Distantly the thunder rumbled, the rain now settled into a steady rhythm. The tree swayed wetly about, sending down leaves and sodden blossoms and showers of water. Fallen leaves spun in wet whirlwinds that never quite made it off the ground. All the birds had disappeared, and all the squirrels. Butterflies wouldn't have stood a chance.

'I don't think I'd have been much good checking them out anyway,' I said. 'I don't know what I'm doing myself half the time.'

'Then it would have been perfect,' he said.

'But I must confess to the thought that you were beginning to stir some of that high-grade stuff into my chicken soup.'

Martin looked shocked, then all at once his good humour returned. 'Your chicken soup!' He laughed. 'My chicken soup I can see might be necessary but your chicken soup never.'

I noticed then that Lobsang was not putting his bundle down, only moving it from one shoulder to the other, so I took him over as if it had already been arranged that he share my room.

I showed him his bed next to mine and he immediately

sank into it with an arm over his eyes as if he had too much sun – or chop suey. I left him there and went back to Martin whom I found talking to Lila.

She was standing on the bottom step of the stairs with one hip out, leaning her elbow on the banister, a small child's fist at her ear as if playing telephone.

'. . . all of a sudden she seemed tired,' she was saying. 'She refused her food, just taking juice . . .'

'I'll go up,' Martin said.

'No. She said for you not to come. Not just now. Later, she said. After she's rested. Om Prakash is with her now, and he will call you.'

'Very well.'

She took her fist from her cheek, hit her mouth with it, gave it a kiss, put it back near her ear.

As she turned I put my hand out and coaxed her with wiggly fingers.

Still holding her fist up to her cheek partly under her hair, she came down off the stair. When she got up to me she stood on my toes. That's the nice thing about bare feet.

I took her wrist and brought it down near my eye. The thumb was tucked inside the fist. I scrutinised it.

'What you got there?' I said.

'Careful! It's hot,' she said, popping her thumb out and touching the ball of it with the pointing finger of her other hand before popping it back in again. 'Mataji's put the whammy on it, I think. Held it for an hour, it seemed.'

'What you going to do with it?'

'Plug it in somewhere and light up all of South India.'

'Do you think it's possible that we have all gone absolutely doolally,' I said.

'Wouldn't that be great?' she said.

'I'm not sure,' I said.

'Let me go,' she said. 'I'm helping Lakshmiben make sweets for Deepavali.'

'Who he?' I said, knowing my cue.

'Ask Martin,' she said, getting off my toes and moving away. 'He knows all the Pavali brothers.'

Next to my chair was one of those umbrellas that collapses into a very short thing. I held it up like a highwayman's pistol, let her get to the door.

'Wait!' I said, pointing at her. 'Pow! Pow!'

'I can't wait until you're twelve,' she said.

'Talk like that ma'am,' I said, trying to speak like Lobsang, 'and you'll get it right between the eyes.'

I flicked at the knob and it exploded open. She shook her head and left. Can you possibly feel better than this? Get grown up? What a laugh! There's hope for me yet.

'What's Deepavali?' I said to Martin when he came back.

'It is a festival celebrating, among other things, the recovery by Rama of his kingdom.'

'The Rama of Harikrishna-Harirama fame?'

'He, the ideal prince, lost first his kingdom and then his wife Sita, the ideal woman, but with the help of Hanuman the lord of the monkeys he first recovers Sita and then, later, his kingdom . . . His return culminates in the Festival of the Lights.'

'Comes at the right time,' I said.

He nodded. 'With lights and fires and firework displays.'

It couldn't be much past midday yet it was almost time for them now. The rain was horizontal, wisps of cloud scudding low in the dark sky. Lightning occasionally flashing, sometimes in sheets, now and then zigzagging right across the sky. The wind and the rain and the rush of the river so loud you couldn't hear the thump of sea.

Somewhere in the house shutters were loose and banging. Om Prakash and Hari scurried all over, checking up, moving things away from the leaks, emptying buckets, laying down long sand-filled socks to contain the water flowing in from the courtyard. Occasionally tree branches or palm fronds came crashing down, and pots overturned. But there was a sense that we hadn't seen anything yet.

'This is really going to be something else, isn't it.'

'It's the same every year,' he said.

'I didn't mean only the monsoon . . . First it's only the dirt and corruption . . .'

And then?, he might have said.

'. . . and then it's the hopelessness . . .'

'And then,' almost definitely this time.

'. . . and then it is the pursuit of the ideal and the celebration of the recovery of the lost kingdom . . .'

Martin sat up straight and looked intently out into the rain.

'. . . with the help, of course, of the king of the monkeys.'

'I'll tell you this,' Martin said. 'If you want to stay as you are, you've got to be always on the alert. You know? Always.'

'Yes,' I said.

'It's as if some force hovers over this land waiting to take advantage whenever it can perceive the slightest chink in the armour. It will take any chance to get in its thrust, will use anything, now matter how mundane, no matter how vulgar, how seemingly irrelevant, will use anybody, no matter how ignorant, how criminal even.'

'Yes,' I said.

'It's the only country I know where the man who wants to avoid the discovery of God is never safe . . .'

Suddenly he looked as if he were vulnerable but we were in too deep for me to take advantage of him.

'It is the fragrance, I think, that's what it is,' he said, 'the fragrance of all those saintly men and women who have walked across the land, taking from it nothing and offering up to it everything they possess.

'It's as much a part of the environment as the roadside dust and burning cow-dung and the monsoon rains . . .'

Hari from the outside and Lobsang from the inside both appeared at the same time. But before they could come close I said: 'I promise not to quote you if you promise not to implicate me.'

'It's a deal,' Lobsang said, giving me five, neither one of us knowing what we were talking about.

Lobsang was wearing my duds, changing his appearance, looking OK although my white Levis stopped at the knobs of his ankles and he almost burst the seams at the seat; my tee-shirt was stretched all out of shape, the motto 'Tonight's the night' like on an inflated balloon.

Hari looked as if he'd just been brought up after spending three weeks counting coral. If I were to draw his picture his ears would be spouting fish.

'Everyone has left,' he said, as if it were something he had personally accomplished.

'How deep is it now?' Martin asked.

'This deep,' he said, holding his hand halfway to his knee.

'Is there any chance,' said Lobsang, 'of the house being swept into the sea?'

'All the chance in the world,' Martin said.

'Shall I set them free, master,' I said, hamming it up, picking up the knife – a curved cutty stuck in a joint – and as soon as he nodded I was out in the wet and slashing away at the last two thongs of the panel. It was done before you could say: hear no evil, see no evil, speak no evil. I swung the panel free so that the monkeys could go over the wall any time they wanted to. But they didn't move a wet finger, nor twitch a wet tail.

'Now we can't get rid of them,' I said when I got back.

It was a little bit like being marooned on the island of Doctor Moreau, though Lobsang said it was more like an Agatha Christie mystery just before the bridge goes and people start disappearing.

'I don't know who's going to be the next victim,' I said, agreeing, 'but if you leave me out, and the monkeys, I can think of at least three good possibilities.'

For a couple of hours the skies had just about emptied. A centie a minute it looked like. Even with the thunder distant we had to raise our voices over the roar of the river and the rattle of the rain.

The sky had turned the colour of damsons and by mid-afternoon every light was on. The low clouds dragged their ragged edges just above the tops of trees; with the wind increasing the courtyard tree swirled about in tremendous movements, pulling the bamboo cage all out of shape. The courtyard seemed a field of smoking flowers.

Lobsang and I had the view to ourselves. Hari, for most of the time, was locked into one or another of the asanic postures in the dark at the top of the stairs, humming to himself, and Lila and Lakshmi were busy in the kitchen. An hour ago Om Prakash had called Martin upstairs and the two of them, the lucky stiffs, had been up there ever since.

Lobsang had been telling me some of his experiences with the seekers at the University of Colorado. He was in the middle of a tale of how his Communications Class was making this movie of the Tibetan Book of the Dead when, suddenly, a row of bells for the maid and butler started to trill high up on the wall, one or two or more of the six always going. Hari, who was passing through when they started, looked jerked out of his mind.

'Bells,' said Lobsang, 'have always been recognised, even in Upanishadic times, as signs which accompany an opening to a higher state of consciousness.'

'Yes,' I said. 'But that was before tubular lights.'

Lila and Lakshmi and little Nataraj came in to gape.

'You've got a full house,' I said.

'I never knew they even existed,' Lila said delightedly.

'Don't you know it, everyone needs their shaving water at the same time.'

'There's no one here but us chickens,' she said.

'Then it's poltergeists.'

'They've never paid us any notice before,' she said, then corrected my pronunciation.

'Someone amongst us is impure?' I intoned. But I cut it out when I saw how unsettled Hari looked.

'Do something,' Lila said.

'Er, right. What you know about electricity, Lob,' I said.

'I know that to change a light bulb,' he said, 'you push it up into that socket thing and twist it so those two little whatsits catch hold on those two little doodads.'

'Is that a fact,' I said.

'Yeah,' he said. 'What you know about electricity?'

'Well,' I said. 'I know about fuse boxes. That's where fuses hang out.'

'Is that so,' he said.

'Nataraj,' I said. 'What you know about electricity?'

He didn't know much apparently for he hid his laughing face in his mother's thigh.

Just then the bells stopped . . . but the lights immediately began to flicker. And outside it was dark.

'Agatha Christie is OK,' I said, 'but I wish I were trapped in some other book.'

'It's time to light the Deepavali lamps anyway,' Lila said. Lakshmi had earlier filled the little clay boats with oil and now she lit the floating wicks and placed the lamps all around the room. It looked better than Christmas. When Lila brought one lamp to my table, I could see the flame shining in her eyes.

'You know what?' I said to her. 'We write songs about the wrong things.'

'We don't tap-dance enough either,' she said.

'When we going to have Mister Pavali's sweets?' I said.

She spoke in Hindi to Lakshmi who went and brought a tray of white things in syrup. We all got one, Nataraj sitting cross-legged and eager with his spoon up and his elbow out as if waiting for the starting pistol.

'Lovely,' I said when I'd taken a bite. It was sweet and milky and a bit rubbery. 'But I don't think mine's quite dead. It's still squeaking.'

The electric light was now more often off than on. Hari had taken advantage of the situation and appeared with two hurricane lamps which he said he would take upstairs to Om Prakash. He did so but was back down almost at once with a serious-looking Martin.

'I'm never one to give up hope,' I said. 'Martin, what you know about electricity?'

'The pole by the side of the river is probably down,' he said.

'Man, is he hopeless,' I said to Lobsang.

'Just don't know the rules,' he agreed.

'In this wind the connection could have pulled loose,' Martin said.

Suddenly I was eager again for the storm. 'Want me to check?'

'There's nothing you can do,' he said, 'even if it remains connected. And it may be live.'

'That's another thing I know about electricity,' I said.

'Don't tie knots in a live wire when you're standing in a river.'

'But you can take a look if you like.'

Lobsang said he'd come too and Lila got busy getting together rain gear and towels for our heads and even a pair of old green wellington boots.

'You can have those,' Lobsang said. 'I'm scared they'll fill up with muck and suck me under.'

'Wellies,' I said with nostalgia as I climbed into them, 'My God, clump, clump, clump, what you doing in India?'

While we got ready as if for an adventure, rolling up our trousers, laughing at nothing, knowing it was not to be taken seriously, I saw Martin quietly climb back up the stairs, this time carrying his doctor's bag in one hand and a stethoscope in the other. Hari also saw him go and I thought at first he'd follow. But he stopped at the bottom of the stairs, looking up.

'I feel like the Creature from the Black Lagoon,' I said in capitals when I was all bundled up.

But it was great. The winds were tremendous, the rain horizontal, every step a struggle. The night couldn't be blacker. The small light from the torch punched out a thin hole in the darkness to show a rock, a fallen palm tree, swirling water, but what it revealed made little sense. Everything looked different with broken branches and bits of bamboo everywhere, and everywhere new streams and miniature waterfalls and rapids. And the noise! The sound of the rushing river and the roaring wind merged into an endless deafening clamour that confused us. And then the thunder started up again. Light and sound exploded at the same instant, the noise seeming to agitate the blue and fragmentary view into unconnected images. For a moment we were lost though only twenty steps from the gate and we couldn't find the footbridge. Then we saw the pole with the wire. The footbridge should be beneath it but there was nothing, only the water rushing past. As we watched the wire, already hanging low, broke and whipped away downstream. We started to pull our end in but it was only about twenty feet long so we stopped and let the force of water uncoil it again. I aimed the torch across the river where the footbridge was supposed to be but there was nothing now visible: no planks, no poles, no wire. Simply – for as long as the beam of light would go – an expanse of rushing black water.

Lobsang made a big gesture with his arm to get us back to the house. Soundlessly I laughed at him. It was just like the movies with two heroes fighting the elements. Together in slop and slither we made it back to the gate and got inside. For a moment I thought we didn't have the muscle to close the door. But we managed, and laughing like loons we were back in the comparative calm of the verandah. How peaceful it seemed. How lovely everyone looked. Lakshmi in her new sari, all reds and oranges, Nataraj like a young prince in crisp white trousers and gold-embroidered kurta, Hari with his bare chest and woppy eyes. And Lila . . .

'You're just great,' Lila said. 'You go out to find out why the light flickers and all the lights go out for keeps.'

'You don't know what it's like out there,' I said, unwinding my towel turban, somehow jubilant. 'Tell her Lob.'

'It's like forty underground trains,' he said.

'It's like some mad monster from the depths,' I said.

'It's like ten horizontal Niagara Falls,' he said.

'It's like some Edgar Allan Poe/Walt Disney Production,' I said, feeling outclassed.

It took us a long time to settle down, I tell you, the storm having got inside us and set up some reaction in that part of us that always prefers it that way. But gradually the natural peace of the surroundings overcame the exuberance, and we settled down.

Nataraj helped, for I remembered the tin grasshopper that Lila had bought for him and I went and brought it out and set it before him. I had to hold his hands the first time until he caught on. But when he was on his own he just took us over with his delight. Sometimes the thing took minutes to get free from its suction and it didn't seem as if he'd be able to contain himself as the tension built up. Then WHANGO! up it went and he laughed and we laughed, the whole thing new each time. We must have done it twenty times before Lakshmi took it away from him. And by that time we were more or less OK inside again.

Lila and Lakshmi spoke for a while together in Hindi and then Lila explained that where Lakshmi came from they sat up all night before Deepavali and sang songs, and that she had asked Lakshmi to sing for us some of the songs they used to sing. So we got out her little box harmonium and she sat cross-legged on the floor pumping it a few times with one hand while she tried out the keys with the other. Lila sat on the floor near her and little Nataraj, looking as if he'd just about had it, curled up against her. Hari came and sat nearby and Lobsang, leaving me the only one in a chair.

She sang for an hour I guess. That's about all I can say. The music wasn't what I'm used to. Nothing tricky. How tricky can you get with a one-handed harmonium? But it was very sincere, you know, and a very sweet voice. As I say it isn't what I'm used to. But it put us all in a very gentle place. After a while we accepted the storm and took no notice of it. I suppose the word for it is, if you'll pardon the word, harmonious.

Then Martin came down the stairs and changed all that. He stood on the bottom step and waited, and for a while no one took any notice of him. But then Lakshmi, in the middle of a song, happened to catch his eye and she just sort of faded out in mid-phrase, the harmonium groaning into silence.

Everyone looked at him.

He put his hand on to the banister and then looked down at it as if to see what it was doing.

'What's up Doc?' I said, some tension in me making me sound just like Bugsie.

'The Mother is withdrawing from her body,' he said.

Nothing happened. For a moment everything completely without movement. Still. And then – wham! Hari was up and racing for the stairs. Martin grabbed at him, got his dhoti in one hand and as he didn't stop, stripped him then and there before diving at him, getting a leg. Down they went together in a frantic tangle. I tell you I didn't think either of them had it in them. They used in ten seconds more energy I'd seen from either of them in three whole days. I mean for a while it was a struggle going on there. You couldn't have choreographed that scene even for a Tamil movie.

Finally Martin got him pinned and Lobsang went and held him and that was that. If Lobsang held King Kong that would be that.

But everyone was shaken up and Martin dabbed at a lip and breathed hard a bit before he said to Hari: 'You are not to go up there. Is that understood? You will stay here until Om Prakashji calls for you. Is it clear? And when he calls you it will mean that he wants something done immediately. Without argument, without fuss, without question. Do you understand me?'

Martin! My God! This was Martin. The Martin with the clamshell-brim hat and the gentle voice and the immaculate doctor's hands. I never would have believed it.

But an answer was too much to expect from Hari just then. He looked sort of unconscious. Lobsang stood back from him but it was a long time before he stirred. Finally he stood up and Lobsang gave him his dhoti and he walked over into a corner and turned his back and put it on.

He wrapped it round, tucked it in, then turned and faced Martin, his hands closed up at his side. He didn't say a word and his face was blank, his eyes dead.

No one else had moved in all this time but now everyone repositioned himself. Nataraj who had been asleep and
had awakened in the struggle cried a bit but as no one paid
him any attention he soon stopped. Lakshmi stood up, re-
draped her sari as if she'd heard nothing much then stood
erect like a queen. Lila was frozen in a kind of dancing pose
looking out at the night, the backs of the fingers of one
hand covering an ear. Lobsang sort of brushed down Martin who was looking at his hands as if to watch for tremors.

'You mean she's dying?' I said.

There might have been a nod. Or it might have been
just a gesture of impatience.

'But . . . what's wrong?' I went on.

'Nothing's wrong,' he said.

'Nothing's wrong,' I said, 'except that she's dying of it.'

It sounded harsh and if I could have brought it back,
I would have. But all he said was, 'She's a hundred years
old . . .'

'But why now?' I said, persisting.

'Physically, you could say, there is very little . . .'

'I've never seen you wriggle before,' I said.

His mouth formed words that never made it past his
lips, until he finally said: 'It seems to be her time.'

'You mean she's choosing to go?' I couldn't let up but I
seemed to be the only one.

'It is not quite like that.'

'Then what is it like?'

Lila turned to me and took my hand and squeezed the
hell out of it and gave me a dismal failure of a smile.

'I don't understand,' I said. 'That's all.'

Lobsang said: 'The death of someone holy is always more or less a conscious act.'

And then Hari started. 'I don't believe it. I don't believe it. I don't believe it . . .'

It seemed to go on for ever, certainly it was going on long after Martin had gone back upstairs. But just when I had got used to it I realised it had stopped. Rather it wasn't audible anymore. But from the way Hari held himself and the way his eyes were and the way his lips moved I got the feeling that although you could not hear anything it was still going on, this expression of his loss and his disbelief, in a silent, inward chant that occupied his whole space.

He went and sat on the bottom step of the stairs and for the next hour he inched himself up, one step at a time, so that when he was finally settled he was perched on the top step of the first flight like some portentous bird. It was dark up there and although down below it was pretty with lights, all the flames wildly dancing, it was the darkness that now seemed to predominate.

The storm did not ease, neither the wind nor the rain. In fact it seemed to increase. The village was managing to set off a few fireworks in celebration of Rama's victory – big bangers mainly with only a few flowering complexities in the sky – but the noise from them was almost lost in the general din.

Nataraj had fallen asleep again, and he was lucky. The rest of us didn't know what to do with ourselves. Our capacity for speech had left us – for a time it even seemed that I had lost the capacity for thought. There was a blankness inside, a shadow of non-comprehension that inhibited the mind's natural ability for working things out. I sat looking at things – the patches of damp spreading along the walls like maps, the flickering lamps, the raindrops dancing in a pool, the water gushing out from the water-spouts – without even the usual critical commentary. The meaning of things seemed to have been extracted. Let go, I said, let go, remembering all the rubbish from those hopeless loopy-dust trip sheets.

Lakshmi brought in an enormous straw basket of jasmine blossoms that she must have gathered before Darshan for they were all dry. She made herself comfortable on the mat with the basket near her and began with a needle and thread to make garlands. For a while we all watched her then Lila sat next to her and threaded a needle and also started a garland. Lobsang and I hung back for a bit but then, together, we also sat down. Lakshmi showed us how to pierce the centre of the flower and we all went to work. I rather fancy that Lakshmi and Lila could have gone quicker, but the basket of blossoms was our life-raft: without it we would sink. And we had a long way to go before we reached land.

It is not difficult making these garlands, but there is something about it that makes you very conscientious. The needle goes in, there; the thread is pulled gently through; the flower tucked in firmly up against the last one; the petals arranged just so. And the fragrance just about knocks you out. The local name for jasmine, I was told, was Purity. A most peculiar idea came into my head.

It was this: you cannot be pure for the love of purity; you can be pure only for the love of God.

It made me a little uncomfortable, this thought, so I made an effort.

'Those lizards,' I said, nodding at the walls where a couple of them were clicking their tongues at each other.

'Geckos,' Lila murmured.

'Yeah,' I said. 'Of all the experiments he's just about the most perfect . . . except for one thing . . . I wish he wouldn't bite off his kid brother's tail and go about with it sticking out of the side of his mouth like a fresh dude with his first cigar.'

Lobsang and Lakshmi made no sign that they had heard. Lila held her work down in her lap and looked at me with a smiling distracted gaze.

'Smart-arse?' I said.

She shook her head, selected a blossom, put it to her lips, then reached over and tucked it behind my ear.

And we went back to sewing flowers.

Time passed of course, you could tell that by the way the storm built up and died down and by the different intensities of the rain and by the fact that finally the noise of the fireworks ended. Once Lila got up and left us to bring a hot drink, a yellow tea without milk and with some kind of spice in it and jasmine flowers floating in it. Once Lakshmi went into another room and stayed there a while and came back with eyes red. Once Nataraj cried out in his sleep then woke up fretful, before almost at once dropping off again. And then Lobsang just sank to the floor next to

Nataraj and flaked out like a weary big buck seal. Time passed; I knew it. I just did not experience it . . .

If the past is no more and the future not yet, how can time be measured anyway when you are trying to calculate from or to that which does not exist? I mean time, if it exists, is now; time if it is anywhere, is near, an extension of what's inside the head . . .

But what happens when, as now, time seems to stop. Does it continue its existence elsewhere, contracted maybe into another dimension or expanded perhaps into another space? When it starts up again will the constellations have moved? If time ceases to be, what takes its place? What does time include and what is not governed by it? What, if anything, is outside it? . . .

O the mind, the mind, with all its impediments which are called laws. Temporary truths, that's what they are, not laws, accurate only within a static universe. An in-time but out-of-date universe, an observable-within-the-senses universe, a limited-by-man's-intelligence universe, a satisfied, grown-up, unevolving, fat-head of an universe . . .

And outside this universe we can achieve immortality can't we, living forever in the moment . . .

Being new to this growing-up business I had to blame everything on it. Adult thought processes, that must be it. It had to be, for nothing like it had ever happened before. But it's all right, I remember, thinking before I passed out. One can get used to anything.

One minute I was there thinking grown-up thoughts, the next I was waking up on the mat, flat out, cold, with

Lila pulling a blanket over me, kneeling there looking very – here we go again – grown-up.

'All right,' I said. Statement not question.

And she answered with a nod. 'All right.'

I pointed up at where two fireflies had come in out of the storm and were playing tag in the rafters. Lila gave my hand a squeeze before she left.

Lakshmi was lying down but with her dark eyes wide and far-seeing; Lobsang was still out or out again, and the child.

The basket was empty of flowers but full of garlands.

Patterns flickered on the ceiling . . . There was something I was supposed to remember . . . The wind moaned about the house, loose bamboo pieces clattered about; there was a lull in the rain, only the water gurgling from the pipes and the drip-drip-drip from the trees. And the roaring of the river.

I remembered what it was. There was supposed to be a sense of loss, and of sadness. I tried to feel again what had so shaken me. But I could not. No sadness was there, no sense of loss. Time already had taken care of it.

# 7

## MILK IN A DOG-SKIN BAG

WHEN NEXT I SAW the light of day it wasn't much, grey and cool and dripping and barely dawn. But it was commotion that caused me to open my eyes, not light. The room was empty before me but when I turned over on a sore hip and looked stiffly over my shoulder I saw the lower half of Lobsang just disappear up the stairs in a hurry with the sound of hasty feet ahead of him. At the foot of the stairs Martin stood with Lila and Lakshmi, looking up.

'At a guess,' I said, handling my sleep-thickened tongue with difficulty, 'Hari must have remembered this time to tuck up his sheet.'

For all the attention I got, I needn't have bothered. The sound of scurrying feet stopped. Then Om Prakash's voice, indistinct, followed by a long drawn out, 'Oyoyo.'

'Has she gone?' I said.

Everyone walked about a bit, looking for their places. Not being able to find them they stopped again where they were, the women looking at Martin.

'Yes,' he said.

Lakshmi raised her hand in front of her face, swivelled

it at the wrist and slapped it against her cheek, keeping it there, as if for earache.

It was quiet now at the top of the stairs but after some time you could hear footsteps and then Lobsang and Om Prakash came slowly down with Hari between them. When they neared the bottom of the stairs Hari stopped, forcing the others to stop also.

'You and your black bag,' he said almost conversationally to Martin.

Om Prakash shook him by the elbow then moved him, resisting, down the stairs and across the room, Hari leaning back, twisting to keep Martin in view, one cheek twitched up as if by a stroke.

'If you'd left her alone,' he said, 'she would have lived for ever.' Just before he was hustled through the doorway they all heard him cry: 'How could she go.'

Martin was like a rock, his face without expression. He placed his palms in the small of his back, leaned back into them, rolled his head in its socket, his eyes on Lakshmi as she climbed the stairs.

Lila plumped a cushion for him, said, 'Tea?'

He nodded, sat down and thrust his legs out before him. Then he closed his eyes and stayed like that without moving until the tea was brought.

There was some for all of us and no one spoke as we sipped it. From the back room we could sometimes hear Hari's voice raised but the words were indistinct even though the emotion was clear. If Om Prakash answered him he must have spoken softly for we couldn't hear his voice. And after some time we couldn't hear Hari's either.

Before we finished our tea Lakshmi appeared on the stairs and spoke to Lila in Hindi. Lila cringed her shoulders a bit into herself.

'Give me five minutes,' she said to her in English. And to me she said, 'Let's see what the river's doing.'

'Right,' I said.

I was up immediately and away, waiting for her outside in the light rain. As we walked to the gate I saw the soaking wet old bachelor monkey climb up on to the wall and settle himself with his head between the bars, peering wistfully down into the wrecked and empty cage.

The wind was tremendous, though perhaps less than it had been when Lobsang and I had gone out into the dark. When we unlatched the big gate it blew in on us and almost knocked us into the bushes and we grabbed one another as we helped each other through the opening.

Outside was a new world, the old one having been completely washed away in the night. It had a new shape to it, this world, a new colour, an entirely different atmosphere.

The river raced swiftly by, wide and brown, not only filling the bed of the old river but scouring out a new and wider course. Part of the high bank had collapsed and on this side it had swept high up the river beach taking away almost all trace of the shrine with its rocks and its pile of flowers. The tip of the island facing up-river had a new contour, had become blunt and rounded; even as we watched, clumps of earth from the bank fell away into the water. Nearby trees, their roots laid bare, leaned out into the river, the current tugging at their submerged branches.

Things, known and unknown, were being borne past in the flow. Among the recognisable things were the bloated body of a sheep or a goat or something, a bundle of clothes, a broken door complete with frame, a bed with four mosquito net poles still in place, sundry pieces of lumber, a red plastic bucket, branches, bundles of straw; on the far side a whole tree slowly turned over and over.

The wind was roaring in from the sea against the force of the river, whipping up the water into white-topped crests. The clouds were ragged, indistinct, breaking up and streaming away inland low over the trees. No one was visible on the far bank doing their morning ablutions as was usual this time of day. There were no signs of birds or scrounging dogs or wayward cows. No sign of life at all. Only the wind and the low sky and the rushing water.

Lila reached out for my hand and our fingers inter-locked. We went along the bank and stood on a rock inches above the brown water. The rain had almost stopped but the raindrops stung with the force of the wind. She tilted back her head and slitted her eyes, opened her mouth, stuck out her chest. I did the same, letting the wind breathe itself into me.

Untouched by anything but the tops of waves for thousands of green miles the wind had come in clean, without nonsense, sweeping away everything loose, everything not in its place, everything old, everything rotten; had come in with the rain like a wet broom sweeping everything away. Even the old smell had gone, being replaced by the smell of that sea in which everything is purified.

'Some blow,' I said, after we'd been thoroughly cleaned out, inside and out.

'The radio says a cyclone is sitting out there,' she said, 'Not sure which way to go.'

I looked out to sea where the horizon was hazy and close.

'But I think we're in the eye.'

'Jolly good,' I said, silly-assing it.

She turned to me, her eyes probing mine as if she couldn't quite believe me. She still had my hand down by her thigh so we were close. But for something that was not quite clear she could have been just some schoolkid still in hair ribbons. Her hair streamed across her face: her eyes, serious, peered through it.

'Listen!' I said, to give me time to follow her mood.

'You listen,' she said, jerking down at my hand.

'OK,' I said.

'Just listen, that's all.' For a moment she looked insecure so I gave her hand a squeeze.

'OK,' I said. 'I'll listen.'

'From now on. Hear?'

'OK.'

While we were still standing there, the five minutes long gone, Om Prakash came out with Hari, each of them holding a bamboo pole to which was tied a white bed sheet. On the sheet in black paint was written a message in Tamil script. They put it down on the ground and started to dig holes for the poles while Lila took me over so that she could read it.

'What does it say,' I said.

'It's to tell them that their Amma has gone,' she said.

She untangled her fingers, turned, and left me. I watched her through the gate before I went reluctantly to help them put up their flapping sign.

While we were tamping down the earth and propping up the sign someone appeared as if by magic on the far bank. But it was an old man and maybe he couldn't see that far for he just stayed there peering across at us. Then a small boy came up but maybe he couldn't read for there was still no sign of comprehension. But after some time the small boy went to get a bigger boy who apparently could both see this far and could read for there was immediate reaction. Before long a couple of hundred people lined the river bank. Just standing there, looking across.

Going back inside the gate I saw Lobsang up in the top rigging like a sailor, a leg hooked at the knee while his hands were free working at unfastening the bindings on the bamboo.

'D'you want a knife?' I called up to him.

He shook his head, tapping one that was stuck in the top of his jeans. Rather, my jeans.

I tested the structure with my hands then climbed up to join him. The cage tilted with our weight on it, leaning towards the house.

'It's for the fire,' he said. 'She's going to be burnt.'
'When?'

'As soon as it can be done. When it starts again it could rain for weeks.'

We untied first the panels at the highest part near the centre of the dome, so weakening its structure. It swayed as we worked, the wind exaggerating every movement. The loose pieces we dropped down into the courtyard, leaving the bamboo in panels wherever possible. It was going quickly but we stopped when a flurry at the gate caught our attention.

Om Prakash was striding towards the house, twisting to avoid the restriction of Hari's grasp.

'Saints are buried,' Hari was saying.

'Amma is to be cremated,' Om Prakash said.

'Her place is holy,' Hari said, doing a little dance. 'We must build her a tomb and do pujas.'

'It is a holy place,' Om Prakash agreed, 'Holy if she is burnt, holy if she is buried.'

'It is not right,' Hari insisted.

'I do what she instructed me to do.'

'But think,' Hari said, with both his hands holding on to him. 'All the people from the village. And from far. They would want her body preserved. She will keep us safe . . .'

'Come,' said Om Prakash. 'I need your help. You must help me officiate.'

Hari's hands dropped. Om Prakash started to move away then came back and took Hari's arm and led him inside.

'I thought all yogis were burnt,' I said to Lobsang.

'Some are, some aren't,' he said. 'There is a tradition for burial, the idea being that the realised man has passed through enough fire already so there is no need for him to do so at the time of his death.'

He went back to his knots. 'But in any case she was never one for tradition.'

'At least it's not much trouble,' I said. 'That's something to be said for it.'

'Not much trouble for whom?' he said. 'It's convenient enough for those left behind. But who are they? Nothing's happening to them.'

'But they are the only ones that matter,' I said. 'You can't do anything for anyone else.'

'Can't you hell,' he said.

'Well like what,' I said.

'I wouldn't know where to start.'

'Start anywhere,' I said.

But he just shook his head.

'I've never done a death before,' I said, when it was clear that he wasn't going to go into it. 'Not experienced it. You know what I mean? Before there were just people who suddenly ceased to be, just went out of my life. Wired-up flowers, borrowed black tie, lace hankies, cold meats and then – readjustment. But I've never felt that feeling of . . . well if not of irreparable loss then at least of irrevocable change. Like if it isn't grief, it'll have to do.'

'In a way Indians don't believe in death,' Lobsang said. 'They're as bad as the Irish with their wakes and their weepings but deep down they are comforted by the idea of the everlasting return.'

'Listen!' I said, but then I remembered what Lila had said, and stayed quiet.

'Comforted, that's what they are,' he said, 'by what they strive to avoid: rebirth.'

I waited, struggling with the knots, and with more besides.

'I guess it's just like a boat without oars drifting away from shore,' Lobsang said. 'At night . . . and someone on the shore letting go the rope – '

'Yes.'

' – knowing he is linked with the one drifting away.'

Far out over the top of the wall I could see the crowd on the far river bank. It had spread out as if waiting for some festivities, for some display on the river, for a procession perhaps of boats like those Siamese affairs all gold and crimson dragons.

'Grief's got no place in it,' he said. Suddenly he took out his knife and slashed again and again through a difficult binding.

'We've got a story of an old sage whose wife had died and when his friends came to visit him the next day found him with a cooking pot turned upside down on his knees, tapping upon it and singing. How can you act this way, his friends wanted to know. All these years living together. She bore you children, looked after you when you were sick, you grew old together. The sage said, would you expect less? When someone is tired and goes to lie down you do not run after them, crying out, disturbing them. She whom I love has gone to sleep in the great inner room. To intrude on her rest with all my lamentations would show nothing of the law.'

Lila was right, I thought. The only man who can say 'Listen' is the man who has something to say.

Hari had been given some ritualistic jobs, something to do with camphor, something to do with incense, something to do with clarified butter, something to do with the scouring of brass bowls. In his quiet way he was making a lot of noise, not enough to disturb anyone but enough so that you could hear if you happened to be anywhere near him. In fact he sounded like the inside of a confessional booth, one voice expressing sorrow and the other with the compassionate words. Myself, I stayed away from him as much as I could for any time I was close to him he went through a performance of pulling in his skirts, cringing into the woodwork and doing the Hindu equivalent of crossing himself.

Lila and Lakshmi we hardly saw, both being for the most part upstairs, and Om Prakash also seemed to have plenty of things to do. Martin had slept the morning but had come and helped after lunch when I went to lie down for five minutes and slept for ninety. By the time I came out again the cage was down, the monkey gone, with some of the bamboo stacked outside the wall but most of it piled, without much hope, to dry under the thatched roof of an outhouse. When we had just about finished making some order of the courtyard Om Prakash came and asked us if we all wanted to have a last Darshan.

Hari was first in line with Lobsang close behind him, queuing up like kids for a free dip.

'I'll skip it,' I said, which stopped Martin from joining the line.

'Give us a few minutes to clean up,' he said to Om Prakash.

Om Prakash waggled his head in agreement and as everyone was dispersing Martin came up to me.

'Last chance,' he said.

'I'm not spooked,' I said, wondering why I needed to say so.

'Have you witnessed death before?'

'Oh sure,' I said. 'Sure. I suppose. Pa, Ma, Grandad – all of them. And I'm getting my quota up these last few days.'

'This may be different,' he said.

'I saw her alive,' I said.

'Take your shower,' he said, 'and think it over. I'd like you to come.'

'OK,' I said. 'I'll think about it.'

Though why I played hard to get I'll never know. Why should I not go, as invited. How could I not go, when asked. It didn't make much difference either way. Yet I knew I would much rather not go if I could find an inconspicuous way of refusing. And I knew that it was not because of a love that had died but because of a love that had just been born. It was like not wanting to go back to a loved place because of the changes that would have taken place there while you were away, spoiling everything.

But I was disturbed, let's face it, by something not in the landscape.

In the bathroom when I looked in the glass I felt as if I were looking out from some ice-sculpture which had been set out in a weak sun and stray wind. I felt suddenly trapped in a world that would not change, in which I was filling up with memories that didn't belong to me. Memories of trying to hang on to something gone, of young people growing up already fearing the hole in the ground, with no radiance anywhere. And memories of another time, where everything was fresh and ageless, when all life seemed one long recapitulation of things known, when you were able to let go into an endless discovery that had no beginning and will have no end.

The afternoon was going downhill towards darkness when we all trooped upstairs: Om Prakash with Nataraj, Hari, Lobsang, me, Martin. I didn't like it one bit, this procession; you expected turnstiles at the top of the stairs. It was indecent, nosy, tourist. At the door I hung back as everyone moved in, but finally I followed.

Everything was different: the light was different with the sun gone from the room; the smell was different, not of flowers but of camphor; the very vibration of the room was different, the quality of immense immobility had changed. Something was missing, no matter what Lobsang said.

I moved on in and Om Prakash lined us up as if for medals. Lila and Lakshmi were sitting in saris like open flowers on the floor.

She was lying on a narrow cot that had been covered with a gold-bordered white silk cloth. She had been dressed in a white gown that reached from chin to ankles and wrists. A white cloth was folded over her feet. Her hands touched each other low on her body. Her colour was almost as in life, her face very little lined, her mouth pouting forward as if in some amusement.

And a dialogue started up within me, with one side saying NOTHING HAS CHANGED and the other side saying NOTHING IS THE SAME. After a while the words changed to EVERYTHING IS THE SAME and EVERYTHING HAS CHANGED. And before long it wasn't a dialogue any more but a kind of chorus, agreeing on principles, the words complementing each other.

Suddenly Hari broke. Sobbing, he threw himself down at the foot of the bed, his hands touching her feet, his head down almost to the floor. Om Prakash moved as if to go and restrain him but Nataraj, looking uneasy, reached up for his hand and Om Prakash gave it to him and stayed where he was. No one else moved and Hari let himself go.

But just as suddenly his sobbing stopped. Slowly he raised his head, almost slyly, and peered up at the Mother over the end of the bed.

'She's not dead,' he said.

Om Prakash freed his hand from Nataraj's grasp and moved forward. He touched Hari on the arm.

'I can feel her alive,' Hari said.

Tugged at by Om Prakash he turned to Martin, coiling himself down to half his size, as if ageing, pointing at him with a crooked finger and with his elbow up, looking at him from under his brows.

'What have you been doing?' he said almost in a whisper, the last word thrust out like a spear.

Lakshmi closed her eyes and dropped her head, touching the spot between her eyes with a middle finger; Lila turned to look out the window. No one else moved a muscle.

'She is asleep,' he said, still in the same whisper.

Om Prakash murmured 'Amma,' and lifted him to his feet. With some resistance, he moved him out of the room. All the way down the hall and all the way down the stairs we could hear Hari explaining how he knew that the living being was still present.

Lobsang stepped forward and prostrated himself before the bed, flat out, forehead, chest, toes and palms to the floor. Just a second then he was up and gone. In, down, up, out. Gone. You felt like cheering. Martin was next, taking not much longer, moving up, dropping his head, touching his heart, turning, leaving.

I could not move. Neither forward nor back. Hey Ma, I said inwardly, this is it. For what it's worth, here I am. This is all I can bring together at this time. It's not much. But take it. I'll never understand this, I'll never understand what you are, what your being here means. I'll never be the same that's all I know. Maybe I haven't changed much, but change is change isn't it? How much change is needed anyway for the course of something to be changed, for the pattern of something to be changed, for the destination of someone to be changed? All I know is that I am different and this does not disturb me . . .

There came then this waiting with everything nice and relaxed and content. And although there were the usual little tugs – do this, say that – they were not insistent, and could be ignored. It was not of course like a usual parting – see you, have a nice day, don't take any wooden pennies – but it was nothing serious either, nothing final. Laughter was near, that was the surprise. And that was the clue to what I wanted. One thing before I go: I want to hear your laughter.

I waited. What else could I do. And it came. Laughter like I never heard, bubbling up within me, aerating the whole system, held back at the lips with some effort, filling every nook and cranny, taking light into every area of darkness, breathing air into every stagnant corner, filling me, enlarging me more to my ordained dimension. A laughter like light, with irresistible force. Everything became laughter; there was nothing else. Everything became delight; there was nothing else. Everything became joy; there was nothing else . . .

From the doorway where I found myself with the knob already in my hand I looked back one more time.

'Don't forget,' I said (or maybe only thought), 'Don't forget what you promised.'

To be with me always.


Before dark we had visitors. Lobsang and I were outside laying out the wooden foundation for the funeral pyre according to our instructions when a boat appeared out of the gloom. It came from up-river carrying men in white and with a boatman in the stern trying to influence its direction with a paddle thrust vertically into the water. Racing straight for the island, bobbing and dipping violently, the passengers popping up and down like puppets in a trick boat, it hit the end of the island with a tremendous schmack, shooting everyone over the bow into the mud. We scrambled to it and held it secure while they sorted themselves out, got ashore. Besides the boatman there were three young men with Brahmin thread and caste marks, white cloths on all of them over the shoulder.

Delighted with their initiative they chattered away but they had no single word of English between them nor Hindi for Lobsang so we gestured them into the house while we helped the boatman tip out some of the water and tie up the boat.

'I wouldn't launch this thing in Trafalgar Square,' I said, picking at the rotten wood with my fingers.

'I hope no one else tries it,' Lobsang said. 'Anyway, you're stuck with them now till the river goes down. From here on out it's the open sea.'

I looked across the turbulent water but it was now too dark to see the other bank where, until a few moments before, you could still make out the crowds of people. What a scene tomorrow would have brought, I thought, had there been no flood.

We went back to the pyre, interlaying branches across the wooden foundation, leaving space for the wood chips and packing.

'All according to rule,' I said, when Lobsang corrected my actions.

'Everything elemental,' Lobsang said.

'Right,' I said. 'And by the look of this pile it's going to be an absolute conflagration.'

'It's got to be big enough to do the job,' Lobsang said.

'Nothing's hidden,' I said. 'That's the unsettling thing. Everything right out front.'

'What have you got to hide?'

'My God, everything, everything,' I said. 'Or so I've always been told.'

'Nothing can be hidden forever,' he said.

'You can try,' I said.

'Well look at this,' Lobsang said, nodding towards the house.

For Martin and Hari were coming out of the gate arm-in-arm. Walking slowly towards us.

But almost immediately I saw that the apparent was not the real. Martin's hand had been pulled through Hari's arm and Hari held him by the thumb while with the other hand he pressed a knife against the root of it with the same gesture you would use to slice away a hand of bananas. Both of them were so concentrated on the thumb and the knife against it that their heads were almost touching and their legs were going as if hobbled together for a three-legged race.

Lobsang hissed his breath out through his teeth and backed away to give them plenty of space. I held out a bamboo pole I had just picked up but I too backed off.

Hari gestured Martin into the boat without giving an inch of thumb. The whole thing was clumsy as hell but the knife was still there when Martin had finished crouching down facing the stern, away from us with his free hand back under the armpit. You could see the barely restrained force of the knife arm just tensed to slash.

Hari jerked his chin, wanting us to step back away from the boat. We moved, but not enough his eyes said. We moved again. And then – impasse. To cut the rope would mean taking the knife away from the thumb. You could see him looking at the knotted end around the bush and looking at us and you could see him considering the risk.

His eyes started on a kind of haphazard route, down and about and up and around, trying to see a way out.

'Hari,' I said.

He looked in my general direction, his eyes not quite in focus. I remembered the action of his open hand and the other sawing at the wrist, I remembered his words: 'I know where it grows,' and involuntarily I backed off another couple of steps.

'Martin,' I said. I was just full of meaningful remarks.

'In the long run,' Martin said to me over his shoulder, 'it might be better if you untied the rope.'

'What's up, Hari,' I said.

'It is her place,' he said.

'We're all visitors.'

'It is my place also,' he said.

'Michael,' Martin said. 'Untie it.' He attempted to lighten the tone of his voice. 'This time I won't have anyone to bail me out.'

Suddenly everything changed, with Om Prakash calling from the gate. Immediately Martin was thrust headlong down into the bottom of the boat and the knife slashed across the rope. And as the rope parted and the boat nosed from the bank and turned with the current everyone went into action: I took a running plunge into the water to try to reach the stern of the boat, Lobsang took off like a hurdler along the river bank, Om Prakash ran straight down into the river to try to head it off, and Hari shot off into the trees.

Martin came scrambling up out of the bottom of the boat fumbling for the paddle as the boat was caught up, gathering speed in the current. When he thrust in the paddle he still seemed unsure which bank to aim for, for the current swept away from us and up against the farthest bank. The boat was already going faster than I was, so I turned back to shallow water near Om Prakash who was up to his waist and insecure on his feet. As the boat disappeared into the gloom we struggled into shore and began picking our way along the bank. We were halfway to the beach before we came across Lobsang knee-deep in water with his hands on his hips.

'Did you see him?' I said.

'Going like a bomb,' he said. 'Paddling like crazy for the other side.'

'You think he made it?'

His mouth turned down at the corners. 'He was sure travelling.'

He came out of the river and we all stood there in the dark, dripping water, looking across towards the other hidden bank. The wind had pretty well dropped by now but the air was still filled with the sound of rushing water.

'It looked,' Lobsang said, 'As if he was getting swept out to sea.'

Om Prakash was like a pillar of stone and when I touched him his flesh was cold as if life had left him. A flurry of bats appeared from out of the trees and for one dreadful moment I thought they were going to cluster upon him.

'He'll be all right,' I said, meaning of course Martin, but his first words showed that his concern was for Hari.

'He is on the edge of the abyss,' he said.

He turned then back to the house and set off, walking faster than Lobsang and me. By the time we had returned he had searched the house and, not finding Hari, had stationed the young Brahmins on the top floor, one each at the top of the two stairways and one outside the Mother's room.

'I am going to look for him,' he said. 'Leave the gate open but . . . watch.'

'You're just about hopeless without your wife,' I said as he was about to leave. 'At least put on a dry wraparound.'

He looked down at his wet lungi, absently wrung out a corner, nodded, and went back into the house.

'Same to you,' I said to Lobsang. 'And from now on we'd better do everything in shifts. But move it or I'll catch me death.'

When Om Prakash came back he stood for a while in front of me as if preparing something to say but he couldn't get it out and gave it up.

'Take a lamp,' I said as he turned to leave, but he shook his head. He paused again after taking a step into the courtyard.

'If the storm keeps off,' he said, looking up into the darkness, 'we will light the fire at daybreak.'

And then he was gone.

When I heard the gate click shut I found myself turning and turning about slowly. The two hurricane lamps, one at the foot of the stairs and one at the inner door, illuminated little beyond their immediate area. Most of the festival lights had been taken elsewhere and the world was becoming occupied by shadows, all moving, all conveying more than they contained.

For with the night had come doubt. Not that independent need to question what you believed in but that weaselly instinct that even lacked the courage of disbelief. The fluttering light of the lamps was dominated by the surrounding gloom. All the dispellers of the dark – the radiance of the moon, the sparkle of the stars – were forgotten. The place was now the domain of night, the time was the time of darkness . . .

I started to shiver in my wet clothes.

# 8

# THE WELL-KINDLED FIRE

'NOW I KNOW WHAT THEY MEAN when they say chilled out,' I said, towelling my hair till I saw stars – or planets I guess they would be for they didn't twinkle.

But Lobsang was somewhere else.

'I don't suppose with a head like yours you ever see stars,' I went on, dumbing it up just to get his attention.

But lack of comprehension didn't bother him none. He didn't give me the time of day.

'It never came up,' I said, getting to what was troubling me. 'Whether he could swim or not.'

'He'll be all right.'

'Though I suppose everyone, just about, can a bit, these days, can't they.'

'He'll be all right.'

'Except Tibetan elders that is. They don't need to worry do they? With all their powers, walking on water and all.'

'He'll be all right.'

It helped some, the repetition, partly because I believed the same myself. But there was still an unsettling tremor in my throat high up under the jaw which had nothing to do with the chill.

'But I'm not so sure about Hari,' Lobsang said.

'He'll be all right,' I said, switching roles, taking his part but with nothing like his authority.

'Think of it! He's had to give up what he perceives as the meaning of life just when he thinks he's found it.'

'He'll be all right,' I said, trying again.

'He feels betrayed or something – what he wanted most having been taken away before he'd really experienced it.'

'He was into renunciation, wasn't he?' I said, 'He should be able to figure it out.'

'Easier said than done.'

'He should be able to figure it out; I'll never be able to figure it out.'

'Well don't look at me.'

'What's it mean, renunciation?'

'Means different things East and West.'

'I'm not partial.'

'It's a tricky business,' he said. 'It starts with looking.'

'What's Hari looking for?' I said.

'How do I know? When you start looking for something anything can come up. And what comes up you have to look at. Don't you? Whether you work it out or push it aside or get swamped by it is something else again.'

'What sort of things come up?'

'Whatever it is you don't want to look at.'

'What's that got to do with renunciation?'

'Well you can only give up something, isn't it, after you've learnt you've got it.'

'But why must you give up anything at all?'

'If you choose one value you must sacrifice another.'

'Is that a fact.'

'Think about it.'

'For how long?'

'If you can only carry so much you've got to put something down, haven't you, if you want to pick up something else. You're got to empty the cup before it can be filled. Even you must have heard that one. After all it was one of your guys who said it.'

I gave a snort.

'What's up?' he said.

'What a conversation for two young punks to be having,' I said.

'One punk, one monk.'

'Two punks!' I said.

'But at least this young punk knows that the other young punk doesn't want to give up anything,' he said.

'Right,' I said.

'He wants it all.'

'Right.'

'And you know how I know? Because part of me feels the same.'

'It does?' I said.

'Sure.'

'How can you say that? Man, you look committed.'

'I'll tell you something,' he said. 'That trip to God's country dropped me way back down the path. Con-taminated me good. I found I loved the world, that's what happened. It's comic, true, and everyone is doing everything wrong, and everyone's settled for pleasure rather than joy, for tricks rather than truth, profit rather than progress. But the world's beautiful, that's a fact.'

'Then why?' I said.

'Why what?'

'Why this way?'

'What way?' he said. 'Why my musty robes and bald head and my beads and my four-thousand-year-old words?'

'Yes.'

'How about this for an answer: I don't know.'

'All right then,' I said.

'They've proved it can be done this way,' he said. 'So it's one way to go.'

'Sounds like you don't want to give it up until you've found another way but you can't find another way until you give it up.'

'Sounds like you're beginning to understand,' he said.

'So you're not sure then,' I said, watching him squirm.

'Look!' he said. 'Not sure of what? I'm sure of what I want; I'm just not sure when I'm going. That's all. Hell, I've just this minute found another possible way. The sunlit path is not a Tibetan thing, you know, so I'm as new to it as you are.'

'But . . .'

'But nothing,' he said. 'You're not going to understand anything by talking to me. If you've got to ask somebody about it ask the one up there who's filled with all that light.'

'But she's dead,' I said.

'Dead, hell,' he said. 'She's an undying principle.'

He was worse than Mickey-Mack, as sure as beans.

'I don't know what's come over me,' I said. 'Question marks are taking over my life.'

'That's India,' he said. 'In America it's asterisks.'

'Om Prakash has been gone a long time,' I said, managing something that wasn't a query.

'It's dark out there,' he said.

The image of the coconut palms in rows came into my mind, row on row, confusing the mind, and two figures in the dark moving within the pattern, lost in it, one calling and listening, the other listening but not answering.

'This is about the time when Agatha Christie would separate us, right?' I said.

'I was just about to suggest I go look for him,' he said.

'What did I tell you.'

'Just a quick look. I'll take a flashlight.'

'That's the way it would go. First you'd stumble over something messy . . .'

'Don't say things like that.'

'. . . and then he'd slip by you and have my tripes out for macramé.'

'Inside your head,' he said, 'must be the original hall of mirrors.'

'And then you'd come back just in time to save Lila from a fate something 'orrible, and throw him off the roof.'

'Didn't you ever read Winnie-the-Pooh or anything like that when you were a kid,' he said.

'You can't change authors in mid-swamp, now can you?' I said. 'I see Hitchcock doing the movie.'

'He's dead,' he said.

'All the better,' I said.

'You know if they've got a flashlight?'

'I'll get one,' I said. And when I found it I tried it out, shook it and said, 'Perfect. See how dim it is and fluttery? Just when you hear someone behind you stepping on a twig it will go out.'

'When I get back –' he started.

'If you get back,' I said.

' – I'll do a puja for you and blow camphor dust into your earholes.'

When he left the verandah all you could see was the legs of my white Levis ticking away into the darkness. But even the white legs were almost gone by the time he got to the gate. Open-kerlick, squeaky-wheeze, close-kerlick. And I was alone with my thoughts.

But Lobsang was wrong really. It was not like that inside my head. Not dark at all. At least not often. And not now. There was just something that loved skirting around the sacrilegious, that wanted to see whether or not the holy would hold up under all the mockery, that just didn't want to admit out loud that there was any light at all inside, or joy. Like now, for example, I had closed my eyes for a moment and inside had flashed an image of water lilies in a still pond. Like Monet. Where do they come from, these pictures, when you would think I would be concerned with images of loss, and concern, apprehension even. I opened my eyes briefly to the sight of lamplight in the dark and closed them again and the picture was still there. A pool in sunlight, still, tranquil, a kind of golden mist over everything, and the lily pads turning,

190

turning slowly, revealing different aspects of the flowers which were white with golden centres. I could have watched them for ever. But gradually the mist thickened around the edges so that it was like looking with a glass through a cloud at a distant and receding place that you suspected was paradise. Before it could disappear altogether I opened my eyes, like to try to keep some of it and not use it up all at once. Inside was that, outside was this. And OK too, cosy and friendly these small lights with all their many shadows . . .

But I needed company.

Mickey-Mack seemed to come out reluctantly, wouldn't unfold properly, and when he was finally out he was subdued and clearly not impressed.

'Am I out?'

'You're out.'

'How can you be sure?'

'I helped you on with your coat.'

'Seems like in to me.'

'You're out.'

'Where out?'

'How long are we going to keep this up?'

'You're asking me?'

'Who else? And that makes four questions in a row.'

'You think I could have a pocket all to myself one day? You have no idea what I have to share my digs with. Tin grasshoppers, bits of fluff, dirty old money.'

'When we get to cooler climes I plan to give you a coat pocket with a flap.'

'All to myself?'

'I was thinking more of a regular room-mate, a sort of left-handed monkey chap kind of fella.'

'All those peanut shells,' he grumbled. 'I'd rather have Andy Fumbles back.'

'Well, that's no problem. He'd be a bit shiny though. And we'd have to call him junior.'

'Exactly like him?'

'Well, improved some.'

'Not too much improved.'

'OK.'

He covered his eyes with his arms, turned his head away.

'She's gone then.'

'In a manner of speaking.'

'I'll miss her.'

'I gather you're not supposed to.'

'She had such . . . intelligent fingers.' He hugged himself.

'Did you know that if you choose one value you have to sacrifice another?'

'So-I-would-presume!' he said. 'But if I have to give up grief then what is the other value I must take up?'

'What comes next is always the interesting part.'

'What comes next then?'

'Beats me.'

'Where's my daisy?'

'With my rose.'

'It shouldn't be out of mind, should it, just because it's out of sight.'

'Out-of-sight! It really was, huh.'

He heaved as if lifting himself out of his trousers, which of course he didn't have on.

'You OK?'

'I'd like to say everything is hunky, but I really have to think about it.' Which was usually his way of saying that he'd had enough for a while.

'Here, I'll take you walkies,' I said, thinking to spook the Brahmins.

So, brandishing Mickey-Mack before me, I got up to go and check everything out.

It was a bit like a movie of a visitation of some creature from outer space who comes with this great hypnotic power or something. At the top of the main stairs was one young Brahmin flaked out with his head back against the wall and his mouth wide and his legs stretched before him, one hand clutching at his wooden beads. I stepped over him and before the Mother's door was the same thing. Out to the world as if he'd been zapped with some electronic wand. Just to check I went down the hall to the top of the back stairs – and there was the same thing. This one snoring even. Some guards!

I went back to the Mother's room and quietly opened the door on to the candlelight and the smell of camphor. Lila, standing at the open window, turned as the candle-flames flickered in the draught but looked at me with no sign of recognition. Om Prakash's wife was stricken like the Brahmin boys outside, her hair a little mussed and with little Nataraj curled into her side. I found myself looking at the Mother to see how she was. She too seemed asleep.

Lila held out to me an expressive hand and I crossed the room and took it and turned it over and slapped her palm with mine.

'Sound of one hand clapping,' I whispered.

'Do you think he got across?' she asked, absently fondling Mickey-Mack's head. ('Mmm,' he went.)

Seeming without a care in the world, I said, 'If you've got nothing better to do – worry.' For a brief moment she closed her eyes and leaned forward until her forehead touched my chin, then she got hold of herself and shooed me through the door as if I were a woolly lamb.

But before she could move away from the door I'd opened it again, giving her my number-one smile. Reaching behind the door I felt for the key in the lock and showed it to her, twisting my wrist in illustration.

Outside I stepped over Brahmin number two, looked down the hall at Brahmin number one, got up on my toes and opened wide my arms, breathing in. I felt I could expand and expand for ever, not getting any bigger, you know, but still somehow managing to cover more space.

I guess it just doesn't have much to do, does it, with outer circumstances. Happiness I mean. It's just something which comes in – or comes down, like those thought-balloons – entering anyway from some place where it has long been waiting. And when it comes it just stays no matter what the outer circumstances, at least until you start to examine it.

What's that? Maybe a troop of jackals laughing in the distance. That's a guess. Creepy. Without much humour in it.

I went down the hall, stepped over Brahmin number three and went up the flight of stairs to the roof. You came out through a door in a kind of shell-like affair that hides the little man with the score in an opera. But the stage was in darkness, complete except for one side where the small light from the Mother's room shone out on to the branches of a tree. For a moment the night was without movement and, but for the river and the croaky complaints from the congregation of frogs, more or less silent.

There were puddles of water on the roof; the parapet was knee-high and wet and I sat on it with my back to the reflection of light, looking into the night. But that isn't the way to say it: there was no looking. Rather it seemed like that interior vision again but later, after the mist had come completely in. Not that the water lilies were gone for good; it only required some word, I was sure, some gesture, to make the mist pull back. It was like happiness, the field of lilies, always there. All it needed was a new way of looking, and once that was mastered you could see them any time you wanted to. Could bring them back any time you wanted to. And not only water lilies. Anything, anything. For nothing was gone for ever . . .

Mother, let me tell you what I've discovered since I've been in India . . . My God, you're laughing before I even start.

First of all: There's more in the world that you can't see than that you can.

Laughter.

Then: What is and is not, isn't always. Rather: both are, sometimes.

Laughter.

And: What is dying for one is coming to life for another.

Laughter.

I mean: Some die at thirteen, right? Some come to life at ninety-two.

Laughter.

For: If I'm still drawing breath it means there's still more to be done.

Laughter.

And: Paradise and Hell are there . . . or here . . . for those who expect it. Rather: when you believe in them, you're in them, one or the other.

Laughter.

Then: We don't go from death through life to death, we go from life through death to life.

Laughter.

For: Although everyone's got different engines, everyone uses the same fuel.

Laughter.

And: Now that you've shown me how to be immortal I'm going to live for ever – even if it kills me.

Laughter.

Finally: Every tree's got a different name, every pebble on the beach, every wave. And all the names mean the same thing: He-who-runs-things.

Laughter.

How about that. For once I got all the lines.

I gave Mickey-Mack a good shake to wake him up and let him have a good look around.

'I bet you've never seen such thick nothing,' I said.

But all he did was swivel his head and say in a low voice, 'Ohoh!' as before me, beyond him, the dark seemed to solidify, gain substance, take form, acquire arms, a trunk, a head.

'Who's that?' it said, the shape. The voice was small and hesitant as it would be coming from a child suddenly awakened in the middle of the night, and finding himself in odd surroundings.

'Is that you?' it said.

'No, it's not me,' Mickey-Mack said, telling the truth. But he said it without thinking, not recognising the risk until it was out and too late.

Hari materialised out of the dark.

'Who is it then?' he said.

'That's a good question,' I said, once again falling back on delaying tactics.

'Isn't it?' he said.

He dropped cross-legged before me, and before I'd realised it had taken hold of my wrist, Mickey-Mack still sticking out of my fist. The reflection of the light from the branches outside the window lit him up some, not much but enough to show his eyes and the white cloth tied around his loins. Enough also to show the blade of the knife he still held in his hand. It was one of the curved cutties we'd used for the cage. He held it with the knuckles on his knee, the blade pointing back in the slicing position.

He didn't look fast, but whatever he wanted to do was done before you knew that he planned to do it. Now he had the knife blade on my wrist, flat, just below where he held Mickey-Mack up into the feeble reflected light. It felt cold, the blade did.

'I'm a friend anyway.' Once Mickey-Mack got started it was difficult to know how to change it.

'You are?'

'Sure. Have you got any enemies?'

'Oh yes,' he said, absent-mindedly jerking a thumb back towards the centre of his chest.

'Are you sure?'

'Oh yes,' he said.

'Who are they then?'

'They are the ones who, when there's light, are dark,' he said.

'What they do?'

'They just want you to believe in what they believe.'

I guess he was right at that. He had enemies. And so did I. On that basis even our best friends were enemies. But I played the chicken and said nothing.

He was holding himself very straight and as I was slouched forward on to my knees our eyes were almost level. But with my back to what light there was I don't think he could see mine.

'Do you know why it is we're always wanting to kill something?'

'No, why?'

'Because we want to achieve the impossible,' he said.

'What impossible?'

'The killing impossible,' he said.

'What you mean?'

'Do you know what it's like to be dead?'

'No.'

'Neither do I. No one does. Do you know why?'

'Why?'

'Because there is no dead.'

I grunted in the Tamil way of encouragement.

'I can kill nothing,' he said.

'Me too,' I said.

'And no one can kill me. Even if I ask for it. Even if I die because of it.'

I tell you, without the practice Mickey-Mack had given me, I don't think I could function in this world. Not as a straight man anyway.

'No one can be killed,' he said. 'You know why?'

'Why?'

'Nothing can die. That's why. Everything is always alive – earth, fire, water, air, everything living for ever, only changing from one thing into another. Even the dead live, dying in one place to come alive in another.'

He reached up with his knife in a big movement, switched his grip, aimed the point at the back of his head and scratched his scalp with it.

'Is that really you M-Mum-Michael?'

'Yes.'

'You look black.'

'We're all that colour when the sun goes down.'

'Except Amma,' he said.

'Yes,' I said.

'She always shines.'

'Yes.'

'And some others,' he said.

'Listen,' I said, breaking down.

'What?'

'Om Prakash.'

'Om Prakash?'

'Yes.'

'Yes what?' he said.

Jesus! We could be going round all night at this rate.

'Is he all right?'

'Isn't he?'

'Where is he?'

'Where?'

HOLY COW!

'Yes. Where?'

'Om Prakashji?'

'Yes.'

'Do you know what he tried to do?' he said. He held the knife out towards me and twisted the wrist. 'He tried to do something but he couldn't.'

'What did he try to do?' I said, the words coming slow through a dry mouth.

'He tried to make me change.'

'How was that?'

'He wanted me not to be the way I was. Why did he ever do that? If Amma accepts me the way I am why couldn't Om Prakashji have accepted me the same way?'

The past tense!

'Do you think I'm crazy?' he said.

'A bit,' I said.

'I think you are crazy too,' he said.

'That's the nicest thing anyone ever said to me,' I said.

'At least you are when you talk to that black thing.'

'Black thing!'

He held up my wrist and shook Mickey-Mack.

'Black thing hell,' I said. 'He's my buddy.'

'Do you know what I did?' he said.

'When?'

'On the beach.'

'What then?'

'I shan't tell you.'

My heart turned over. But almost at once he went on.

'It was very dark,' he said. 'I could just hear him. He was moving through the trees, saying Om. Saying Om Namo. Saying Om Namo Shivaya. So I could follow him even when he wasn't stumbling about and stamping on sticks. Om Namo Shivaya, he said. Om Namo Shivaya. So we went all over the island like that. He going Om Namo Shivaya, me following the sound. There was nothing else, over and over. Om Namo Shivaya. And then on the beach he stopped walking and sat down, right on the wet beach, me right behind him, him not looking. Maybe he knew I was there. It was very dark but I could see him clearly against the breaking waves. Om, he said. Om Namo, he said. Om Namo Shivaya, singing it to the sea. He and the Mother, both singing together . . . I was right all along, you know. She wasn't gone.'

'And then,' I said.

'And then?' he said, sounding surprised. 'What then?'

Realising my mistake I held my tongue between my teeth. But it wasn't easy when we weren't going anywhere except in circles and me badly wanting to know.

'Om Namo Shivaya. Om Namo Shivaya. Om Namo Shivaya. Om Namo Shivaya. Om Namo Shivaya. Om Namo Shivaya. Om Namo Shivaya. Om Namo Shivaya. Om Namo Shivaya. Om Namo Shivaya. Om Namo Shivaya. Om Namo Shivaya. Om . . . Om . . . Om . . .'

'What does it mean?' I said.

'Mean? He was speaking to Shiva.'

'I mean in English.'

'Oh in English. It doesn't mean anything in English. Shiva doesn't understand English.'

'He does too,' I said.

'He does?'

'Sure.'

'How d'you know?'

'Man,' I said, 'he even speaks English.'

Hari snorted.

'In fact,' I said, 'come to think of it, Om Namo Shivaya is English.'

Although no sound came out of him he jiggled about like jelly on top of an old refrigerator.

'What does it mean then?' he said when he had calmed down.

'You mean in your language?' I said. 'Oh I don't know what it means in your language.'

'I suppose,' he said, after some thought, 'he must know all languages.'

'Well, I don't know about Tamil,' I said. 'But he sure as hell knows English. Why, they all do – Krishna, Rama, all of them guys. BBC Victoria-plum English . . . And I'll tell you something else. They're even learning Chinese.'

'You sound just like you do,' he said, 'when you talk to that black thing.'

'Don't keep saying Black Thing. He's Mickey-Mack.'

'M-Mum-Mickey-Mack. She gave him a daisy.'

'Did you see Lobsang after?' I said, hoping to slip a quicky past him.

'Lobsang?'

Forget it, I thought, forget it.

'Then the four of us came back,' he said. 'Lobsang, Om Prakashji and me – '

The four of us, he'd said . . .

' – and the Mother. Like the three of us now.'

Air kept coming out of me, coming out of me and I found myself slumping forward, chin almost to my knee.

'And then Lobsang went in to change his trousers because he fell in the river again and Om Prakashji came upstairs and went into Amma's room. He had to knock because the door was locked. I think he's still there with Amma.'

'That Lobsang,' I said. 'He only falls into the river when he's wearing someone else's trousers.'

But he'd switched off and turned in, his head dropped so that his face was hidden. He let go my wrist and held his left hand up, palm turned in and with the point of the knife he seemed to be drawing a design on it.

When he came out of it he kept his head down. 'M-Mum-Michael, do you sometimes feel you've lost some part of yourself?'

'Not me,' I said.

'I feel a part of me is missing.'

'Not a part,' I said. 'But sometimes I get the feeling that all of me is missing.'

'All?'

'Hello, hello, anybody home? Nothing. Just a stupid answering machine.'

'Not that,' he said. 'A part.'

'What part?' I said.

'M-Mum-Michael, do you like me?'

Right now he was as sharp as a TV razor blade and as quick as a shot in the bum so I had to give it some thought.

'Yes,' I said finally. 'But then at the moment I like everybody.'

'Everybody?'

'Just about.'

'M-Mum-Michael . . . I'm frightened.'

'What of?'

'I don't know. It's this part of me that's lost.'

'What part is it?'

'I think it's the heart.'

'It's a bad part to lose,' I said.

'Isn't it,' he said.

'But then it's a hard part to lose, too. I can't really believe you've lost it. It's like your car keys . . . er, bicycle key. You've just left it somewhere with your change. After a while you'll remember where you put it.'

'You think so?'

'No one loses his heart like that,' I said, sounding more confident than I thought I could be. 'If you did everything would stop.'

'That's just what it feels like,' he said. 'Like everything has stopped. And I can't remember anything of the time when I had it.'

'Can you remember Amma?' I said.

'Yes. I remember that.'

'There then. That proves you haven't lost it.'

'But that's all I remember,' he said.

'As long as you remember that,' I said, 'nothing can get lost for good.'

'That's right?'

'Sure . . . What was it like when you were with Amma.'

'Like before it all started . . .' he said, his voice lovely with wonder.

'That's nice.'

' . . . and like it will be after it all will end.'

'I guess that's why we call her the Mother,' I said.

'That's why I call her God,' he said.

'Well,' I said, really sharp.

'They say we are all God,' he said.

'I've heard that too.'

'But I never understood that.'

'Neither did I,' I said.

'But I understand her being God,' he said. 'The light comes down into the dark . . .' He put the knife down by his side then stretched his arms up and wide above his head and then pulled them down and held his hands like blinkers at the sides of his eyes. '. . . and everyone can see by it. Some can see a lot. Some not. For me . . .' For a long moment he stopped speaking and held the backs of his hands against his eyes. 'For me it was enough to blind me to everything . . .' He took his hands from his eyes and held them in namaste at his throat.

'Can't she laugh though,' I said.

'Laugh?' he said. 'Laugh! She laughs?'

'I mean,' I said, back-pedalling, 'she makes everything light.'

'Light?' he said, puzzlement filling his voice.

'Well, I guess she gives different people different things?' I said. 'Me, I can't go long without a good laugh.'

'I can't imagine Amma laughing,' he said.

He didn't sound as if he could imagine laughter, period.

I folded up Mickey-Mack and put him away. He didn't have the last word.

When he got up he left the knife there on the parapet. And when I followed so did I. Together we went down the stairs into the dimly lit rooms.

# 9

## THE CEREMONY
## OF THE FLOWERS

COMING FROM THE UNCERTAIN LIGHT of the smoking lamps I thought we'd be coming out into the still-dark but by the time the procession had got outside I could see day was breaking, darkness gradually being leached out of the air leaving the landscape without colour.

But for the stumbling boatman behind me cocooned in a blanket I was last in line; ahead, carrying the bier, went Om Prakash and Lobsang and Hari and the three Brahmins, followed by Lila alone and then the rest of us after-you-no-after-youing. Eleven of us. Or, as Hari would say, twelve. Out in the courtyard our bare feet pattered on the cold stone slabs, finding their way by themselves round the puddles. Someone coughed, someone muttered, someone went oops-oops, as they manoeuvred through the gate.

There was no rain but the air was thick with moisture, little wind but the air was heavy with the change into day. The river, now flattened out, had the sense of urgent discharge; over it hung a layer of mist which wisped uncertainly up the river bank among the wrecks of riverside trees. Above the mist the far bank could be dimly perceived, but without detail. Everywhere water dripped, trickled, ran, leaves ticked. Frogs, in paradise, gave out their muted alleluias.

The swamp smell of the river was gone, the mouse-and-muck smell of the village, the punk-and-pepper smell of India, all gone. It smelt instead seaweedy, resiny, sandalwoody. The day was new, that's what it was, un-formed, virgin, unviolated, ready for anything.

The festival clay lamps were set out about the pyre in a circle, each one two steps from another. The small flames, steady in the motionless air, shone back from the polished surface of the brass pots in which were set yellow-budded branches from the courtyard tree.

The pyre, chest high to Om Prakash, was neat with interlocking wood; tufts of straw and bunches of casuarina needles stuck out from all the interstices. When they lifted her high I went to the other side to help them put her down. She weighed about as much as a wet winter coat. The top of the pyre was arranged like a boat and when we lowered her into it only her head and chest could be seen above the sides. Smoke from blocks of incense smoulder-ing on lumps of charcoal swirled about us.

Across the river on the far bank an occasional match flared, perhaps also for incense, or maybe just for bidis. They can't see much from there I thought, but then as long as they know she is where they look they'll be satisfied.

Everyone but Lobsang was in white. I'd never seen Lila in a sari before. She had the end pulled up over her head like a pietà. With Lakshmi she was tucking white flowers round the Mother's face. The three young Brahmins stood back, close together like a chorus, lips going, eyes turned up like poached sparrows' eggs. The boatman hid behind them, peering out as if just waiting for someone to question his presence. Nataraj, interested in everything, absently arranged and rearranged the contents of his trousers. Hari had his folded hands up as if propping up his chin, his head locked back to the limit of its hinge. Lobsang and Om Prakash stood a bit apart, one like a thick totem, the other stiff in a terrible new dignity.

Close by, almost at the water's edge, a small oven had been fashioned out of a biscuit tin and mud. A fire glowed there, having been lit some time before. Some grain or something was cooking in it. Now the three Brahmins started their business, became absorbed in the act, kibitzing each other, holier-than-thouing, one-upping, dibbing and dabbing, the whole bit. Cere-monious.

As day began Om Prakash went up to the fire with a bowl. Oil was what he had and he was anointing her. He took his time, being thorough. When he had finished he pulled up the cloth to her eyebrows, leaving still visible a fringe of flowers at her hair. Then he lifted two logs – heavy by the way he struggled with them – and placed them with care across the chest and thigh.

I noticed then at my feet a red velvet bug the size of a child's fingernail; bright as a flower it was, the colour of some rare Victorian garter. You're up early, I think I muttered. It went on about its business, legs scrabbling over infinitesimal obstacles. Suddenly I was caught, who knows how, transfixed. For there it was, this bug, in an entirely different consciousness, its sensory equipment conveying to it an entirely different universe, an illusion, complete within itself, unlike anything imaginable. The real differing from the real only to illuminate a new reality. Vibrant with energy, an uncomplicated mass of unfathomable complexities, a concentration of absolutely unlimited potential, there it was, at the moment without movement, absorbing and reflecting some indestructible glory, revealing in that insignificant speck of colour the same presence that was in the sun or the sea or the stillest, whitest light. Suddenly I was linked to it, that was the astonishing thing, linked to it, and linked to this presence, I and it and all things living, moving or still, webbed together for as long as it was needed, for as long as it was willed . . .

The main thing is not to feel loss, isn't that it, for there is no loss; not to accept less, isn't that it, for nothing can be taken away; not to believe that diminution is the way of life, isn't that it. For as he said: she is an undying principle. What we must understand is that what we cast abroad like seed perpetually renews itself, what we let go is only a symbol of that which stays behind, or comes again, what is always there, inside . . .

Always. That's it. What's that image of eternity? About the big rock and the little bird?. . . There was this rock a hundred miles high and a hundred miles wide, and once every thousand years a little bird would come and clean its beak on it. Well, when this little bird finally wears down that big rock so that there's nothing left that would be like the passing of one day in the life of the eternal. . .

The mantras were still going on. They'd taken the food out of the oven and had scooped it out on to a platter. What else they'd done with it I had missed. It wasn't much between eleven, I thought, just a taste all round. Then one of the Brahmins, saying his piece, lifted high the plate, stepped into the river . . . and ceremoniously . . . tipped the food . . . right into the water.

Wow! Such laughter!

Om Prakash was winding straw-rope to a green stick, binding it tight before dipping it in oil. When he called Lila over to him it looked for a moment as if she wasn't going to go. But she did finally, taking up the stick and holding it out for the end to be touched with fire. A soft, yellow flame unfurled like a banner.

Raising her free hand she placed the back of it like a blinker at the side of her face, turning her head away. Om Prakash, standing next to her, took her by the elbow. Together they started to walk round the pyre. Now and then she stumbled, the flame wagging about. Her face, partly hidden, was as white as her sari. Round and round. Seven times? Then coming to a stop: a few shuffling steps closer. Pause. Then Om Prakash moved to her other side, guided her hand, circled the flame over the body near the face.

My heart begins to pound, my breath stops in my throat. I turn away. The mist on the river, thinning, still probes up the shore. The landscape is grey, bleak, without life. I turn back.

Suddenly Om Prakash says something to Lila and she thrusts down with the torch, moves a step and thrusts again. And everything is obscured by a curtain of slow white smoke . . .

It ever was, and is, and shall be, ever-living fire, in measures being kindled and in measures going out . . .

And then my heart stops pounding, my breath is sweet again in my throat. And the day grows wings.

Without flame the smoke swirls and presses down upon the earth, swirls and billows out . . . and then ignites, burning with a mother-of-pearl flame. The smoke turns back within itself; the flames whiten into bloom, unfold. Stones change their colour as they dry. Every blade of grass, every leaf on every bush winks back light. You can see the day catch fire before your eyes, firelight spreading over the desolate waters, eating up the mist. The very air becomes afire with sacrifice. Never, never again, will there be the same darkness.

As if generated by the fire the wind starts up. It roars into the flames and crackles, chimes as in an Easter wind. A smell of autumn, of harvest. A smell of honey. Sparks fly. Ash falls upon the waters.

The sheet has fallen or has burnt, revealing the face. As if encased in ice, the ice itself aflame, she, untouched, seems ensorcered. Even the flowers about her head still look touched with dew. Before her the air shimmers as if everything is about to shift into another dimension, every-thing falling away through an invisible barrier into an unknown world. For what here burns? I, we, everything, every part of us is afire. Here, now, aflame. That is the gist of the new fire sermon.

And as I watch, rehearse, fearful of this shift, this barrier, this new dimension, my mind escapes me . . .

The fire leads in to the way that leads out; it is the only illusion that destroys illusion. It perfumes the night with its accomplishments; the day flourishes in its promise. Sometimes seen as the envisioned tree or as the cosmic bird or as the first opening flower of the midnight sun the fire is born from the wintry waters and from the summer stone. And when the sacred grass is strewn the fire becomes what it must become – the offering of all clarity . . .

For when the highest flame dies into the ruby, the ruby consumed into the ash, what is left is what is given back, enspirited . . .

The guest-wind sings the flame and pursues its many forms while the ghost-wind, instinct with knowledge, summons up the force and all is consumed except the force itself . . .

And all is the burning, for all is the master, the fire in the wind, all, all is the burning . . .

I don't know how long Om Prakash had been trying to get my attention. When I stepped up to him he took my arm and guided me to Lila. (She still had one hand up to her face, her chin tucked into a shoulder, looking away from the fire.)

'Go in and wait,' he said, turning us away towards the house.

I gave a small tug to her sari and Lila dropped her hand from her face and came with me like a child. But at the gate she turned and looked across the river at the crowd of people on its bank.

'Do you think he's there?' she said.

I raised both arms above my head and waved them about. Immediately a figure responded with the same gesture.

'Well,' I said. 'I guess he's earned his rowing blue.'

Almost sleepily she raised a hand and moved it like royalty. Then, reaching across and over the top of her head as if for a fancy frisbee shot, she pinched an edge of sari with her thumb and fingers and lifted it back to uncover her head. Shaking loose her hair she glanced briefly, intently, at the sky. Then after a last glance at the fire she walked through the gate with my hand in the middle of her back as if to stop her from falling over backwards.

'Wait for me in Amma's room,' she said.

The door had been propped open and all the windows were wide. From the outside I could dimly hear the chanting winding down, other noises taking over: crows waking up and seagulls already complaining, frogs just about having croaked themselves out. The river sounded now merely like a steady wind in the trees, the seas like distant gunfire. Inside all was quiet except for the sound of Lila's bare feet padding down the hall to her own room; a click of the door, a scrape of chair-legs, a slide of drawers, and then the complete silence which left me alone in the middle of the room searching for some trace, some remnant of Amma's presence. But there wasn't anything concrete: no photographs, no clothes, no shoes, no personal knicky-knacks.

Nothing was left of the needs of her daily living: a table with stumps of candles and an incense holder peppered around with ash, a ladder-back chair set before it; a small chest with my rose upon the lid (the only flower in the room). The chair with arms in which she had sat when she received me had a cushion on it with another on the floor before it, both imprinted with her form, body and feet. Covering the space between the bed and the armchair was a faded carpet, a desert colour figured with rose and evening blue. Dropped on the carpet near the armchair was one of those long diaphanous scarves that can be crumpled up in one hand. White. I looked at it for some time, listening to interior instructions which I finally ignored.

Can you imagine a film taking in everything, no voice-over or anything, the camera taking its time going everywhere in a room for what seems like for ever, looking, looking, recording every irregularity of surface, every change of light, every hint of emptiness? Can you imagine? I'd have trouble with it. Too much of one thing being like another thing.

Yet I was like that. As if trying to record something so that some time later I could play it back. If I wanted. But it was a very ordinary room. No atmosphere to it, really. Just very still. There was nothing in it that I could record that was worth remembering. Except her.

I moved to the window and two geckos who had been querulously confronting each other on the water-stained walls, tails swirling in slow motion challenge, pattered away across the shutters seeking advantage in the cracks of the old wood. Just like us, I thought, easily spooked, never content unless there's some hole to hide in. The thing is that there's no place so small, is there, that something can hide in without something else being enclosed with it.

From the window you could not see what was going on down there, but with smoke drifting past sound came from the crackling fire, smell from the burning wood.

Lila, changed into Levis and loose top, called from the doorway. She was holding a loaded tray and I went to take it from her. There was a pile of sliced bread, yellow jam, peanut butter if you can believe it, two big bowls of curds, a child's hand of bananas, a couple of wrinkled yellow apples, one lemon, honey in a saucer, butter, a tin of condensed milk with holes punched in the top.

She looked over my shoulder as she handed the tray to me. Seeing the white scarf on the floor she went and picked it up, crumpling it, holding it to her face, breathing through it.

'Hers,' she said, as if she thought I couldn't work it out.

She put it over her head, something ceremonial about the gesture, wound it once round her neck, letting the ends hang down her back. She looked round the room as if for the last time, pursed her lips, nodded.

I followed her to her room and she indicated the floor near the window when she saw I couldn't decide where to put the tray. Then she was gone again. But before I set out the cups and saucers she was back carrying a stove, a kettle and, for the toast, a funny thing two foot long look-ing like a tin fly-swatter.

She pumped up the stove, lit it and adjusted the flame, put the kettle on.

Then, sitting on her heels and lowering her voice she said, as if continuing a thought: 'It's the first time I'm not going anywhere . . . I used to take my 4 o'clock tea in to her . . . ever since I was old enough to handle a tray . . . I'd chatter and she'd listen . . . sometimes she'd take a corner of toast . . . even lick her fingers for the butter, if she noticed I was looking at her . . . Nanda called it my buttered-toast sadhana.'

I waited for more and tried to coax her on but that was all she wanted to say.

She moved her feet and was going to sit back but I insisted she accept my hand and we went to sit on the floor by the window, leaning over the wide sill, both of us tucking our chins into the corner of our arms, touching from shoulder to elbow.

We could see over the wall to where the ceremony was still going on. The flames were out, smoke rising straight, the fire now like a sunken casket of jewels. Everyone still seemed to know what it was they were sup-posed to be doing, everyone moving round, clearly it was complicated.

Hari, getting in the way, was surrounded by an array of empty Horlicks jars and empty jam jars and condensed milk tins with the tops off, as well as with other contain-ers including a couple of ketchup bottles and what looked like an old-fashioned inkpot with a hinged lid.

Two white pigeons clattered down to the top of the garden wall, pigeon-toeing it, cooing away.

Suddenly a tremendous sigh came up out of my body, uncalled, unfelt, meaning nothing, a body-reaction only to some only partially understood thing. A reaction though none the less.

I buried my head in my arms, close to losing it. The thing is . . . I'm not sure any more what she said to me. Something about immortality, I think. Immortality, for heaven's sake! I have trouble with thinking about the rest of the day. And about always renewing yourself. Now I'll never know what other crazy things she'd find to say. She's gone. Can you imagine gone? It couldn't have been longer than five minutes yet it seemed forever. Saint whatyoucallim must have had a similar experience because he couldn't understand it either. I guess I'm never going to get my buttered toast sadhana now. She changed my life, that's what she did. I'm never going to be me again, never be able to say 'listen' any more. A once-in-a-lifetime experience is just not enough, is it, for one lifetime . . . Sorrow, I guess, is only a metaphor. As death is.

Oh, I don't like one bit these grown-up thoughts. They go round like a bug in a box. With never a way out.

Lila ruffled my hair. I think just in time. Otherwise I'd have gone under. I sat up, trembly but dry-eyed. She was back nestled in the crook of her arm as if she had never moved. But how come someone can breathe out so much without breathing in?

A dragonfly came and landed on the back of Lila's wrist. We both looked at it without moving, close up with crossed eyes, saying nothing. A metallic blue it was, whopping great eyethings, bandy-legged, tail way up, wings quivering.

Not moving her lips, Lila finally said softly, 'They start life as nymphs.'

'Nymphs?' I said softly back, copying her with the lips. 'Who do?'

'They do,' she said, nodding at the dragonfly. 'Underwater.'

'Go on!'

'They've found fossils of them . . .'

'Fossils?'

'. . . two feet long.'

'Dragonflies!'

'In Kansas.'

'Oh, in Kansas,' I said.

The dragonfly took off.

'I can believe anything about Kansas,' I said.

Beyond the wall where the Darshan crowd had gathered you could see the monkeys beginning to come out of the trees, spreading out in their investigations. The grove seemed rumpled, like my hair, really messed about.

Hari, seeming impatient, lined up his jars rearranging them in size, their lids already off but each lid next to its corresponding jar. He kept turning his hands as if he were rehearsing the opening of a walk-in safe.

Om Prakash came near him and hunkered down at the remains of the fire. Taking out a handkerchief he placed it over his hand like a magician. Poking about in the ashes with a twig he hooked up some fragments and placed them in the cloth.

Hari thrust an open jar at him but he ignored it, collecting his bits. Then he turned away and carefully and slowly walked into the river. When the water was up to his knees he stopped, lowered the hand with the handkerchief almost to the water and let go all but one corner so that everything plopped into the river.

Hari immediately began to shovel ash into a jar.

And as if at a signal Lakshmi threw a garland of jasmine into the river where it was immediately taken away by the current.

It was over.

Lila made some movement as if to push herself away from the window sill. I put out a restraining hand.

'Did she speak to you?' I said.

She looked off as if to avoid my eyes.

'I mean day to day,' I said.

'No,' she said.

'How did you ever manage to get things done?'

'You somehow knew what she meant.'

'Never a word?'

'Not until the last day.'

'What she say then?'

She looked way off and I thought at first she wasn't going to answer and would let it go, leaving me not satisfied. But finally she spoke.

'First she said, "Lila," and that was surprise enough even after you in the morning. But I managed to say "Yes," though she didn't seem to hear me. After some more time she again said "Lila," and I said "Yes" as before. Thinking it was a game I went along smiling and saying "Yes."

Happy enough just to hear her speak. Her voice, rather indistinct, saying the same thing and I with the same reply. Though each time it seemed to take longer to get out the response . . .

'Finally, when I was all there . . .' she blew out a lot of air with her cheeks full like one of those cherubs on the borders of old maps, kindling the winds over unknown seas. Her tongue went over the lower lip making it glisten.

I intended to wait her out but after a couple of minutes I gave in.

'And then?' I said.

'Then she gave me my instructions.'

'What she say?'

'Dance.'

'Uh?'

'She said: dance.'

'I guess that's clear enough.'

'I suppose so.'

'Did you do it?'

She looked a bit unsettled.

'She had her eyes closed.'

'Well,' I said. 'If you've got to dance, you've got to dance.'

She wiped her nose on the back of her hand and sniffed.

'Hey, look!' I said, to change the subject. The air was becoming filled with winged insects, termites I guess, coming up out of the wet earth, fluttering about just any-oldwhere. Thousands of them. And brahminy kites, maybe a dozen of them, getting into position like a squadron of dive-bombers. Then they began to swoop down low to pick up the insects out of the air with their feet.

'With their feet!' I said. 'Can you imagine? Though the way I am now I'm so hungry I could catch stuff with my ears.'

The kettle was beginning to whimper, letting off a thin column of steam. Lila got free and took down a teapot, warmed it very proper, spooned out tea, poured in the water and put the tin fly-swatter on the stove.

'Pour the tea,' she finally said, more or less coming back. 'The lemon's for you.'

'I've never been mother before,' I said, pouring, the tea going all over the shop as I realised that I'll never be able to use that word again without considering what I meant by it.

'I think I'll have it milky,' I said, recovering.

'Well you can't have butter,' she said.

'I'm all right now,' I said. 'Really.'

'Maybe,' she said with just a twitch of a smile. 'But there's only enough for one.'

It took a long time to make the toast and each batch was eaten long before the new ones even began to brown. She gave me one bite of the last piece after she'd buttered it and it was like the stuff they feed to upper-class angels on Sunday. We drained the pot, wasted the apples and all the bananas and with moistened fingers fought for crumbs on the empty plate.

When we finished she piled everything on the tray and pushed it away. ('For the ants,' she said.) She wiped her fingers on her Levis, shook herself, and looked for a bit on the scene below.

'Let's go down,' she finally said.

Going down the stairs I surprised myself, remembering my psalms, singing out, 'Our God shall come and shall not keep silence . . .' It stopped Lila in her tracks, I tell you, so I went on taking advantage, remembering everything, the words, the tune, everything, the feel of the surplice, the smell of the cassock, everything.

'There shall go before him a consuming fire and a mighty tempest shall be stirred up round about him . . .'

Lila was as serious as my old vicar, at least until I got to the bit about whereas thou hatest to be reformed when she gave me a look. But as soon as I finished she turned and went on down the stairs.

'Hey!' I said. 'You're supposed to say amen.'

'Amen,' she said over her shoulder.

'Not Yey-man,' I said. 'Aaaah-men.'

'Aaaah-men.'

'Right!'

'You sing just like Mickey-Mack,' she said, giving me her back.

'You should have heard me,' I said, 'before my accident.'

The courtyard was quiet and empty, but the wind was rising again. As I followed Lila I turned and stood where the monkey cage had been and looked up at the house. It was dark with water stains; pools of water stood everywhere, everything still dripping. Everything you touched, doors, chair backs, tables, were wet as if the moisture seeped from within. Every item of cloth was damp.

The squirrels were back, their tails as eloquent as ever, and the birds with their what-to-do bird language. Already I missed the commerce and complaints of the monkeys. But no Om Prakash, no Lobsang, no sign of Lakshmi or little Nataraj. No Hari yet. As I say, quiet and empty.

The ground was patterned with leaves and twigs and termite wings and was marked where they had dragged the broken branches along the path and through the gate. To the river I suppose. One big branch, split and splintered, hung down from the tree only partly severed. The thatch of the mud hut was roughed up. Some of the tiles from the top of the wall had been cast down and broken. Bushes lay on their sides, looking as if they'd never rise again. But the upset pots had been put aright and the space round the sitting area had been swept.

While I lingered Lila had gone on through the gate. Finding herself alone she came back. She saw me waiting, looking up, so she came up to me, searching my face for that which was fast losing its camouflage. She caught hold of my ears and gave them tugs as if they needed realigning.

'Hey!' I said. 'My aunties say that that's what you have to do to see if you're done.'

'It feels a bit wobbly,' she said. 'Does that mean you're done? Or not?'

'Part of me is overdone,' I said, 'and part of me is half-baked.'

She moved her hands to frame my face. 'Are you all right?' she said. I tried out my first grin of the day. The first that was at least ninety per cent genuine anyway.

Then she gave me a hug. A real, real hug – what you might call a real home-made thing, fitting her head into the corner my shoulder made with my chin. Her hair smelt of . . . I don't know what it smelt like. My experience of those kinds of great smells is sort of limited . . . I blew into it to see it fly up.

Coming out of the courtyard gate, I saw that almost all of the people on the other side of the river had left. Except for one man, alone, who sat on the very edge of the embankment. Thinking it might be Martin I tried out my made-up semaphore but got no response. Maybe his eyes were closed.

The river, almost red, was still full of rubbish. It moved very fast. It flowed ten paces closer to the gate than it did yesterday. You would never know that there had ever been a footbridge.

The fire was more or less out; wisps of smoke only. And just faint traces from the slabs of incense. Lobsang sat facing the wind and the river. His eyes were open; he looked as if he had just said goodbye to someone who had left on a boat. Om Prakash faced the other way with his eyes closed. Hari had taken away most of his jars and bottles but was still scraping about with a big spoon in the detritus of the fire. The young Brahmins were strictly union: there was no sign of them.

Lila walked past the pyre without a glance. She stood at the edge of the river and picked out the marigolds that she had tucked into her hair: she closed her eyes and brought the flowers for a moment to her bosom. Then, after briefly bringing them to her lips, she dropped them into the water.

They shot off, twirling in the current. She started to walk along the river bank trying to keep pace with them, and I went along. But they were going faster in the water than we could walk on the bank. We stopped near the beach and watched as they were carried out to sea where the river was spreading its colour. Even after the flowers were lost from view we stood there facing the wind.

At least I've found the sea, I thought. You had to laugh, hadn't you. The source was something else again. And the water pumps would always be there.

Lots of damage had been done to the grove; papaya trees and coconut palms and bananas seemed decimated, trunks flattened and stripped-looking, darkened. The monkeys were examining them. We walked among them and they didn't seem to notice us. At least they didn't bare their teeth or anything. Familiarity must breed contempt, huh? To coin a phrase.

'Hello there,' I said to one old fellow who gave me a look . 'He used to be a neighbour,' I explained to Lila.

'It doesn't look as if he recognises you,' she said.

'He wasn't there very long,' I said.

The monkey wrinkled his forehead at me and moved his lips. But he didn't speak. He simply turned his back and looked out to sea as if he were expecting a delegation.

'He looks a bit like Mickey-Mack with a head cold,' I said.

But you know what? You never know what's going on inside anybody's head, do you? Everybody . . . everything's got a life of its own. You know? Monkeys, houses, people. So you mustn't interfere. They know best. Puppets even. Well, perhaps not puppets. Puppets lead a dog's life. Never with an idea of their own. Doing anything for a laugh. Gestures severely limited. Never getting the girl in the end. Words getting put into their mouths. And then there are those dippy names they get stuck with, names that don't have any dignity at all to them. Mickey-Mack, for Pete's sake, and Andy Fumbles! And then there are those smart-arse puppet masters with their set-up questions . . . But even then they have a way with them, those puppets. They often seem to get their own way, don't they?

Surreptitiously Lila snuck her arm round me and seemed to feel along my hip, sending something inside going pitter-patter pitter-patter. But all she was doing was lifting Mickey-Mack from my back pocket. She took him out and slipped him on to her hand as if she had done it before. His arms shot up.

'Hey!' I said. 'You look different.'

'I feel different, I tell you,' he said. He dropped his chin into his armpit. 'There's something new in me.'

'How is it?' said Lila, 'that I've never seen a lady puppet?'

'There's no such thing,' said Mickey-Mack.

'Wouldn't you like a girlfriend?'

He moved about a bit. If he had legs you would say he was shuffling his feet.

'You could share a back pocket.'

He crossed his eyes. Now how was he able to do that?

'All the little ones would have your hair.'

'We would need more hands,' I said.

'Annapeg, that's what she'd be called. Annapeg Mac-Gillicuddy. We could call her Mrs Mac for short.'

'Look at that,' I said. 'He's at a loss for words. Who would have believed it. You're bringing out another side of him.'

'He's bringing out another side in me,' she said.

She tucked him under her chin and his hands came round her neck.

'I don't think you understand,' I said. 'He only gets to do bits I don't get to do. I can do that bit.'

'You can?' she said.

'Easy. With a bit of practice. I'm a quick learner I am . . . and as for you,' I said to Mickey-Mack, 'you can get put away for a long time for things like that.'

I took Lila's wrist and rolled him down like a rubber glove, ignoring his cries of 'ow! ow! ow!'

'Aaah!' she said.

'It's OK,' I whispered to Lila but loud enough to reach the back pocket, 'just joking.'

The wind now was in fierce gusts. We walked down out of the broken trees on to the beach, squidging our bare feet. The sand was dark from the rain and shiny with mica, full of those tiny conical shells.

Everywhere along the width of the beach were long strands of brown seaweed.

She gave a jump and landed with her heels on a pod. It popped. So I did the same thing but slipped on the slime. She caught hold of my hand, and for a while we were like a couple of sand fleas. Pop. Pop. Pop. Pop. Holding hands, sometimes changing direction in mid-air, jerking each other about.

A dazzle of lightning ziggy-zagged across the sky, down over the edge of the world. The thunder slowly rolled around, the returning storm taking its time. The wind was really acting up. You couldn't see where the sea and sky met. Far out was the black sea and above it the black sky. Far out the sea was confused but close in the waves were white-topped, climbing over each other in their eagerness for shore.

The sandbar seemed to have gone and when the waves hit they just exploded on the beach, shelving out the sand.

'Here comes a great big whacking whopper,' I said, raising my voice over the wind.

The wave broke, absolutely booming up the beach, pushing a quivering ridge of yellow spume over our feet. A seabird flashed down along the edge of the water as if it were being sucked down into the curve of the next wave.

'You would have to be a complete dum-dum to try to swim in this lot,' I shouted. 'Now wouldn't you.'

Nothing. Nothing at all. Except a very, very small smile. And her feet changing position as if the earth was moving. The wind almost blew her over so she had to do a couple of quick steps to keep her balance. She turned so that the wind parted her hair down the back of her head, her face covered.

'You look like you belong here,' I shouted.

'What?'

'On a rock. With a tail. Singing.'

'What?'

'You look OK.'

She shrugged, shook her head.

But the wind . . . My God the wind!

Suddenly exhilarated, I shouted at the top of my voice. 'You know something? Today's my birthday.'

I had spoken just as she was about to do something, go into some action which was stopped by my words. She froze as in great surprise, one arm gracefully out from her shoulder, palm up, hand towards me, half turned.

'It happens,' she shouted, her face bright.

I took her hand as the wind in a flurry of rain blew her hair back across her eyes. She closed her hand tight over mine, moved her shoulders, dug her toes in the wet sand.

Then, nodding some instructions, she did a couple of steps and I followed, camping it up.

As the rain came down out of a tumultuous sky, we were off, dancing, dancing, down the roaring beach.

## UNCUT DIAMONDS a selection of new writing
## Edited by Maggie Hamand

Vibrant, original stories showcasing the huge diversity of new writing talent in London. They include an incident in a women's prison; a spiritual experience in a motorway service station; the thoughts of an immigrant cleaning houses; a child's eye view of growing up in sixties Britain, and a lyrical West Indian love story. Unusual and sometimes challenging, this collection gives voice to writers whose experiences are critical to an understanding of contemporary life in the UK, yet which often remain hidden from view.

Featuring Nathalie Abi-Ezzi, Pam Ahluwalia, Michael Chilokoa, Steve Cook, Belgin Durmush, Alix Edwards, Nick Edwards, Douglas Gordon, Donna Gray, Fatima Kassam, Denese Keane, Aydin Mehmet Ali, Dreda Say Mitchell, Stef Pixner, Katharina Rist, Anita Tadayon, Monica Taylor, Pamela Vincent, Joy Wilkinson.

£7.99  ISBN 1 904559 03 4

## ANOTHER COUNTRY
## Hélène du Coudray

Ship's officer Charles Wilson arrives in Malta in the early 1920s, leaving his wife and children behind in London. He befriends a Russian émigré family and falls for their governess, the beautiful Maria Ivanovna. The passionate intensity of his feelings propels him into a course of action that promises to end in disaster. First published in 1928, *Another Country* is beautifully written, its prose is fresh and undated, and its themes of exile, love and betrayal are just as relevant today.

H. du Coudray (Hélène Héroys) was born in Kiev in 1906 and spent her childhood in St Petersburg. Just before the Revolution, she escaped first to Finland, then Sweden, before arriving in England at the age of twelve. *Another Country*, written under a pseudonym while she was still a student, won the 1927 (Oxford and Cambridge) University Novel Competition. She wrote three further novels and a biography of Metternich. She died in 1971.

£7.99  ISBN 1 904559 04 2

## ON BECOMING A FAIRY GODMOTHER
## Sara Maitland

'These tales insistently fill the vison'—*Times Literary Supplement*
'Stay curious. Read Maitland. Take off'—*Spectator*
£7.99
ISBN 1 904559 00 X

Fifteen new 'fairy stories' breathe new life into old legends and bring the magic of myth back into modern women's lives. What became of Helen of Troy, of Guinevere and Maid Marion? And what happens to today's mature woman when her children have fled the nest? Here is an encounter with a mermaid, an erotic adventure with a mysterious stranger, the story of a woman who learns to fly and another who transforms herself into a fairy godmother.

## IN DENIAL  Anne Redmon

'This is intelligent writing worthy of a large audience'—*The Times*
'Intricate, thoughtful' —*Times Literary Supplement*
£7.99
ISBN 1 904559 01 8

In a London prison a serial offender, Gerry Hythe, is gloating over the death of his one-time prison visitor Harriet Washington. He thinks he is in prison once again because of her. Anne Redmon weaves evidence from the past and present of Gerry's life into a chilling mystery. A novel of great intelligence and subtlety, *In Denial* explores themes which are usually written about in black and white, but here are dealt with in all their true complexity.

## LEAVING IMPRINTS  Henrietta Seredy

'Beautifully written . . . an unusual and memorable novel'—Charles Palliser, author of *The Quincunx*
£7.99
ISBN 1 904559 02 6

'At night when I can't sleep I imagine myself on the island.' But Jessica is alone in a flat by a park. She doesn't want to be there – she doesn't have anywhere else to go. As the story moves between present and past, gradually Jessica reveals the truth behind the compelling relationship that has dominated her life. 'With restrained lyricism, *Leaving Imprints* explores a destructive, passionate relationship between two damaged people. Its quiet intensity does indeed leave imprints. I shall not forget this novel'— Sue Gee, author of *The Hours of the Night*